sourcebooks
fire

an imprint of Sourcebooks, Inc.

Title:	Sleeper
Author:	MacKenzie Cadenhead
Agent:	Nicole James Chalberg & Sussman
Publication Date:	August 2017
Category:	Young Adult Fiction
Format:	Trade Paper Original
Trim:	5.5 x 8.25
ISBN:	978-1-4926-3614-4
Price:	$10.99 U.S.
Pages:	336
Ages:	12 and up

D0375611

Also available in ebook

Title:		
Author:		Isabel ande Scavenberg
Agent:		Nicole Jones ... Chalberg & Sussman
Publication Date:	August 2017	
Category:		Young Adult Fiction
Format:		Trade Paper Original
Trim:		5½ x 8¼
ISBN:		978-1-492-63614-4
Price:		$10.99 US
Pages:		336
Age:		14 and up

Also available in eBook

Dear reader:

At Sourcebooks, we talk a lot about how books change lives. For sure, that is an important part of why I became an editor. And I'm proud to say, those are the books we're publishing at Sourcebooks Fire.

We are passionate about finding narratives with authentic teen voices that create—and validate—the teen experience in all of its diversity. We're looking for dynamic storytelling that engages teens and makes them want to read our books, then turn around and share those books with their friends. Because we want our books to be the stories, the characters you remember.

Over the last few years, Fire has grown immensely—and not just in the number of titles that we are publishing. We're receiving more starred reviews, more award recognition, more inclusion on state reading lists. We are broadening and deepening our reach in the young adult market, and in doing so, we're creating breakout successes. We are proud to be the publisher of Marieke Nijkamp's *This is Where it Ends*, which was a number-one read on Netgalley, an Indie Next pick, and spent more than six months on the *New York Times* Bestsellers Young Adult hardcover list (even working its way to number one!). We are thrilled that Natasha Preston's most recent novel, *The Cabin*, was launched onto the *New York Times* Bestsellers Young Adult paperback list, where it joined *The Cellar*, her debut. And we love getting feedback that our books have made an impact on readers, like Juno Dawson's *This Book Is Gay*, narrative nonfiction that explores gender and sexuality and which received a starred review from *Booklist*.

The list of accomplishments is long and stretches beyond the bestsellers lists. And we couldn't have done this without you. Reviewers, book buyers, librarians, educators, *readers*—you have all helped us connect our authors' work with an audience. So thank you for being part of our growth, and here's to all of the new milestones to celebrate in the coming years. We hope this book changes your life.

Annette Pollert-Morgan
Editorial Manager
Sourcebooks Fire

sleeper

MacKenzie Cadenhead

sourcebooks
fire

Published by Sourcebooks Fire, an imprint of Sourcebooks, Inc.
P.O. Box 4410, Naperville, Illinois 60567-4410
(630) 961-3900
Fax: (630) 961-2168
www.sourcebooks.com

Library of Congress Cataloging-in-Publication data is on file with the publisher.

Source of Production: XXXX
Date of Production: XXXX
Run Number: XXXX

Printed and bound in [Country of Origin—confirm when printer is selected].
XX 10 9 8 7 6 5 4 3 2 1

For Phinn and Lyra

chapter one

· ·

If you ever see a door hovering in the middle of a misty, gray fog, don't open it.

In fact, no matter how adventurous you're feeling, or how curious, or how baffled you are by that freestanding door floating in the void, promise me that you'll run in the opposite direction.

In other words, don't be an idiot like me.

The door isn't anything special. Three horizontal panels, distressed white wood, greening brass knob. It's nothing to write home about. But its sudden appearance triggers Christmas-morning-like excitement. Nothing else is happening. I mean, literally nothing. I'm all alone in this ethereal fog. It's been hours since I went to bed. And I am bored. So the sudden appearance of the door is a thrill.

I reach out to turn the knob, and it doesn't once occur to me that what lies on the other side might not be the golden ticket. So when the door doesn't budge? I want in even more.

As I stare at my nemesis, growing more and more desperate to get inside it, my thoughts turn to Gigi MacDonald, captain of my lacrosse team, queen bee to all us wannabees. Any time we drop a pass or let another player get a fast break to goal, she relentlessly runs drills until we get it right. But her favorite motivator is the football team. "You want them to think we're weak?" she'll scream until this little vein pops on her forehead. "Or are you gonna show them that real athletes do more than just run until they hit something?"

The question is rhetorical. But tonight?

I face my opponent. Channeling every football player who's ever scoffed at women's athletics, I take a step back, lower my shoulder, and ram the door with all my might. It flies open, and I fall.

Into...

Black.

Silence.

Chest-compressing airlock.

A stinging wind needle-pricks my face as a deafening FWAP, like the amplified-times-a-million fluttering of butterfly wings, beats against my eardrums, and I'm sure they will burst. My mouth drains of all moisture. I blink and I blink and I blink and I blink. It's all I can do to see anything against the slapping wind in the darkness. I am being swallowed into nothingness.

Until...

I'm not.

My blinking eyelids reveal a flipbook of images: arthritic branches leafless in the moonlight; a rocky path; the color green.

And then I land, face first, in a mountain of crunchy brown leaves. I lie still, inhaling the crisp autumn air that tickles the inside of my nose. Raising myself onto my elbows, I brush away a leaf that's tangled in my thick, dark hair. I've come through the looking glass, but I totally know this place.

I am in the nature preserve behind the Horsemen's football field. In front of me is the Stump—what remains of the massive oak tree that the town cut down when I was ten. I know it now as the favorite late-night hangout spot for Irvington High School's cool kids and a monument to some personal firsts. Not only did I try my first beer here, but it's also where an upperclassman soccer star gave fourteen-year-old me my first kiss. (The beer may have been an acquired taste, but that kiss was like coming home.)

Tonight though, the Stump is deserted. Leafless trees canopy overhead, and a bright full moon plays hide-and-seek between branches. Twigs crunch under my feet as I move over rocks and roots, seeking out a random course that soon becomes an actual path. I'm dressed only in a tank top and boy-short hip-huggers, the slumber party uniform I went to bed in. I rub my arms for warmth. "Always the fashionista," I chide myself. "Never the weathergirl."

I follow the path obediently, trying my best to ignore the goose bumps that have turned my skin to sandpaper. By the time I jump at the particularly loud crack of a twig snapping under my foot, I've wandered deep into an unfamiliar part of the woods.

"Shhhhh," whispers someone directly to my right. Every molecule of my being tenses. Beside me, leaning against a tree, is a shirtless boy with sun-kissed brown hair and four-out-of-six-pack abs, watching something on the other side of where we stand. He is tall, taller than me by a foot at least. Though his shoulders are broad, he's lean, his width easily framed by the thick trunk of a maple. He's got that effortless shaggy short hair that curls at the edges and a long, slightly off-center nose that's all the more intriguing for its character-building crookedness. It's like a wobbly arrow that bursts forth from a prominent brow and ends pointing at some seriously kissable lips. An enjoyably clichéd shiver ripples through my still-tense-but-now-in-a-good-way body. I'm psyched for the companionship but more so that said companion is hot.

He looks over at me, his Oz-green eyes sizing me up before they return to the subject of their stealthy surveillance. Then he reaches out his arm, providing a perfect me-size opening against his chest.

For the first time, I hesitate.

When you're here, in this place, you generally don't waste much time with contemplation. Why would you when there's no such thing as consequence, no final exam, no why or what were you thinking? Here, there's nothing but now. So it strikes me as odd that I have the sudden urge to cover up. Am I feeling shy? Why, when none of this is real, am I embarrassed that the space between this half-naked wood god and a giant tree trunk is the only place I want to be?

I tell my subconscious's conscience to shove it and take a step forward. As I inhale this dream guy, I forget everything else. His intoxicating odor of Dove soap and all-American-boy sweat beckons to me like one of those finger-shaped scent streaks from Scooby-Doo. I slide into place against him.

His chest is warm, but my shivering doesn't stop. I turn my face up to his and smile. He doesn't so much as glance down at me, fixated *instead on that spot beyond us. I wonder what could be more compelling than a scantily clad girl leaning against his chest.*

So I look.

In the center of a clearing, spotlighted by the impossibly bright moon, lies a fawn. Her eyes are wide and her breathing shallow. An arrow protrudes from her side.

"The wound's fatal, but it'll take a while for her to die," the boy says.

I feel a sob build deep within me, but when I open my mouth, I don't cry out.

"I know what to do," I say instead.

Suddenly, I am running into the clearing. I place one hand on the trembling deer's chin and the other on the opposite side of her head. In her surprise, she struggles against me, and I lose my grip. But she is also wounded, groggy, and I use that to my advantage.

I wrestle the animal still, pinning her with my legs. My absolute certainty that this mercy kill is the right thing to do gives me strength.

The boy at the tree calls to me, telling me to stop, but I won't—I can't.

The deer's eyes widen.

My hands return to her chin and forehead and lock in place.

I prepare to snap her neck.

"No!" the boy shouts. "Wake up!"

Everything freezes. The woods disappear. The wind stills. The deer vanishes, though I can still feel her against my hands. I ask, "What did you say?"

I don't get an answer. The boy is gone, and new sounds engulf me, muffled at first.

Someone is screaming.

"Sarah! Stop! You're going to kill her!" a familiar female voice shrieks. I blink my eyes, flickering myself back to reality. No longer am I looking into the blinding late-autumn moon; instead, I see the recessed halogens of a suburban basement.

I lower my gaze and take in the room where two of my best friends are staring at me. Tessa's the one shouting, "*Stop!* Sarah, you have to *stop!*" Amber is clutching her pillow, her jaw almost unhinged in shock. I feel something struggle against me, trying to free itself from the restraints that my limbs have become to hold it in place.

No, not something. Someone.

Gigi, the boss of us all.

She is sobbing. She trembles against my iron-clenched hands, which are locked firmly on her chin and forehead. About to snap her neck.

Crap, I think. *Not again.*

chapter two

· ·

I honestly don't know what her Greek tragedy is," Tessa says as she stirs a container of ranch dressing with a carrot stick. "Gigi's known how to cover up a mark on her neck since the seventh grade."

"True," I agree. "But these bruises are a little more intense than a Tommy Murnighan hickey. Besides, it might be the trying to kill her part that's really got her ticked."

"Eh, potato, potahto." Tessa bites into her carrot, and the loud crunch startles the staring freshmen girls seated at the table opposite us. They giggle as they pick up their trays and scurry off.

"I've got to give it to you, Sar. I didn't think you could get any more popular. It's like, if being a hot, superstar jock made you homecoming queen, being a homicidal maniac added a sex tape."

"With the football team," I say.

"And the pom squad," she coos. Then her smile inverts,

and her eyebrows pull together. Quietly, she adds, "Still, I think Gigi's being way harsh, trashing you around the Quad and banishing us from her table. It's not like you meant to hurt her. She has to know that."

I sigh. Tessa's a good friend. My best, actually. Her determination to support me through the aftermath of this past weekend's horror is both unsurprising and more appreciated than she'll ever know. Thankfully, she's a floater, automatically cool enough to straddle multiple social groups and somehow always remain above reproach. No one's coming after her for sticking with me. But while I sincerely appreciate her blame-the-victim routine as a kind attempt to boost morale, I'm having a hard time keeping up the *que sera, sera* façade. It's been three days since I attempted manslaughter, and my victim has shown no signs of accepting my not-guilty-by-reason-of-nocturnal-insanity plea. Though I know I'm to blame and that Gigi didn't ask for any of this, part of me is shocked that I've been so unceremoniously dumped.

Gigi and I have been friends since our peewee sports days. While we share a passion for free Sephora makeovers and I've no doubt she'd be the first to check an opponent who crossed me in a game, I'm starting to wonder if our BFF status may have been somewhat circumstantial. I mean, when we're on the field, we're the dynamic duo, telepathic in mind and body. Our opponents spend half the game trying to break us up. But it never works. Because out there, we're one.

Off the field, however, there's no *we* in *clique*. In Gigi's little army, I'm a good and appropriately ambitious soldier. I've never considered a coup. Thanks to the skeletons in my closet, I've always felt most comfortable basking in the reflective glow of her blinding sunlight, getting just enough heat to maintain my tan without the threat of a third-degree burn.

But I'm also not a pushover or a lackey. Put me on the field, and I'll murder my opponent. Take me to a party, and I'll prance-dance just seductively enough to make all the boys take note. I like the sweat and the muscle ache and the burning oxygen that stings my lungs when I push my body further than my own brain thinks it can go, as much as I like the power that comes from staking claim to my feminine mystique.

But if I'm being honest, sometimes I get caught up in the moment and push back against my place in the pecking order. Like winning the AP Latin award Gigi thought was in the bag or dating the Horsemen's star quarterback. Suddenly, the line between coconspirator and competitor blurs. She forgets to invite me on a weekend trip to the mall, or I'm left out of a group dinner at the Alp. Suddenly, there's not enough room in the car that's going to the Saturday night rendezvous in the woods.

When those moments come, I prostrate myself before the queen quick and do whatever I can to reclaim my place in her shadow. Because, with a single mom working multiple jobs to keep my life normalish, a dad who's hasn't sent me a birthday card in years, and the really weird stuff I do in my sleep, I have enough drama on my plate. Why would I threaten the most stability I have in my life by crossing Gigi?

I guess that's the thing about drama though. No matter how

hard you try to avoid it, when it finds you, there's nothing you can do but hope it ends in a marriage and not a death.

As I look across the lunchroom to where Gigi, Amber, and my other former friends ignore me from a slightly elevated counter, I'm realizing that the answer to my circumstantial friendship question is yes.

I watch as kids from the upper social syndicates stop by to offer their sympathies—jocks, student council members, even a few of the young teachers seem to be jumping at the opportunity to make it into Gigi MacDonald's good book. And why shouldn't they? The poor girl was attacked in her sleep, nearly murdered by someone who was supposed to be her friend.

Meanwhile, the less-than-beautiful people, the silent majority of the IHS student body, smile at me with awkward approval. That my actions were unintentional doesn't seem to matter. Within hours of the attack, there was an Instagram account revealing details from the stolen police report and leaked photos of a battered, makeup-free Gigi, the fresh bruises on her neck and collarbone red and raw.

While most of the social media response was sympathetic to her, with plenty of people immediately condemning me as a monster, the growing number of likes on the RIPGigi Facebook page and Twitter feeds hailing the #psycho@theslumberparty pointed to a far more disturbing trend. The disenfranchised had finally found their voice. And they were calling me a hero.

Knowing Gigi, it's this insubordination that enrages her the most. My having challenged her social autocracy might be even worse to her than the actual threat of death.

"You know, Tessa," I say pathetically. "No one's mad at you. You weren't excommunicated. You don't have to slum it with me."

"Are you kidding?" she says as she jabs me with a carrot stick, her long, russet-brown fingers contrasting with the ghostly glow of the ranch dressing. "And miss my opportunity to be the inkonsequential Kourtney to your killer Kim? No way, sister. I'm sharing in your interrogation-room spotlight! Besides, we should enjoy it while it lasts. Come college acceptance letter time, some stressed out senior's bound to off himself and steal your thunder."

"That's a little dark, Tessa," a husky male voice chimes in. "And maybe not the perspective Sarah needs right now."

Jamie Washington. Star quarterback, student council member, honor roll recipient two years running, and a bit of a savant when it comes to sucking face. Tessa once said that if Michael Jordan had a baby with Michael B. Jordan, it'd look like Jamie. I don't disagree, which makes being his ex that much harder.

"Hey, Sarah," he says with such legit concern that my whole body tenses, fearful of the breakdown that's bound to overtake me if I give in to this kindness. "Okay if I join you?"

I clench my jaw and shrug as he sits. I know Jamie is doing me a favor by being seen with me this morning. His support will bolster the anti-Gigi outliers and make the popular fence-straddlers second-guess their witch hunt, which is bound to drive Gigi nuts. But she won't ever call him on it because, like Tessa,

Jamie is beloved. He's Switzerland. Solid, loyal, and sincerely kind. He never misses an opportunity to support a friend in need, even if it's only been a semester since said friend broke both his nose and his heart. The former by head-butting him in all my sleep stalker glory after we accidentally passed out while watching a movie. The latter when I dumped him in the it's-for-your-own-good aftermath. Though we've remained on good enough terms, I'm not his typical lunch date. He's just a good guy making a very public show of support. God, it would be nice to collapse against his chest right about now.

"Come on, QB1," Tessa interjects, tactfully filling the silence. "You know what they say. All publicity is—"

"Good publicity," Jamie dutifully finishes.

She ignores his rolling eyes. "It's like we share the same brain," she says and swoons. "Are you sure we're not related?"

"Only by high school drama," I say brightly, resisting the urge to play damsel in distress. "As the best friend and compassionate ex of the sleepwalking whackjob, you two officially share my shame."

"Oooh," coos Tessa. "We're like that movie my mom rents whenever her latest boyfriend bails. We're best-friend outlaws Thelma and Louise. And Jamie can be a young Brad Pitt."

"Wait. Didn't they drive off a cliff into the Grand Canyon?" I ask.

Tessa smiles and nods.

And with that, my resolve goes splat. I drop my head onto the table.

I've spent no more than a millisecond indulging in self-pity when I feel strong fingers weave themselves between strands of my hair as they gently massage my scalp. My body tenses.

"Just give it some time," Jamie counsels. "Everything will go back to normal soon enough. You'll see."

"Right. Just like it did with us," I grumble, effectively killing the moment.

He pulls his hand back. "It will," he repeats without looking at me.

I sit up as he takes two squashed tuna fish sandwiches from a beat-up paper bag. Though I should be feeling bad about making a nice moment awkward, I'm suddenly more focused on the fact that somehow, Jamie's unwavering words have given me a little bit of hope. Maybe he's right. Maybe everything will be okay. After all, if anyone has a right to hate me, it'd be Jamie, and here he is, rallying me with his support.

He takes a bite of his sandwich, inhaling half of it in a single chomp. With a full mouth, he adds, "You just gotta cut Gigi some slack. She deserves a little space to process."

I glare at him. Effing Switzerland!

"What?" he asks. "What'd I say?"

"Tessa takes it back," I snap. "You are so not Brad Pitt. You're more like that awful husband Thelma has to escape from. Or worse: you're the cop who makes them think he's on their side but totally screws them over!" I turn away from Jamie and tightly cross my arms. "You are no longer invited to drive into the sunset with us."

He looks to Tessa for help, but she's already on her feet. "Sorry, friend," she says as she scoops up her tray. "You're on your own. Sar, I'll meet you in the hall. I need a hit of caffeine if I'm going to make it through the industrial revolution. Ta, lovebirds."

Tessa scuttles off, leaving Jamie and me to sit in stony silence. I feel his supersize hand touch down gently on my shoulder. I spin around so fast that I knock it off. "I can't believe you're defending Gigi," I hiss.

Jamie looks like he's just thrown an interception. "I'm not defending her," he offers. "I'm only saying that—"

"Gigi. Gigi MacDonald?" I steamroll over him, unable to stop myself from vomiting out all my pent-up frustration at this undeserving target. "You know, the girl who's torturing me, telling everyone about what an evil freak I am, forcing our friends to choose sides?" I lower my voice. "Did you know she's giving out details of my disorder? Talking about how I do things in my sleep, saying that I need to be chained up at night. She's trying to destroy my life, and you want me to just lie there and take it? Well, I've never been good at lying still, Jamie. You of all people should know that." I stare at him, my hands clenched in tight fists.

He holds my squinty glare with soft eyes as he waits for my breathing to calm. "I'm not saying I'm cool with how Gigi's treating you," he says. "It just seems like she's freaked and maybe needs a little time to be okay with what happened."

"You didn't need any time to forgive me for hurting you." I sound like a pouting child, even to myself.

Jamie takes a moment to consider this. "I knew you weren't yourself," he says finally. "Gigi will figure that out too."

I look away, suddenly unable to stomach this kindness, because I know that the reason Gigi will never come to the same conclusion as Jamie is the same reason why I broke up with him. Being unable to control my actions when I sleep *is* me, and that's something Jamie will never understand. I'm dangerous, and whenever I forget it, bad things happen.

The night I hurt Gigi, I hadn't had an episode in weeks. It was the final evening of the New England Indoor Lacrosse Classic tournament, and we'd placed second overall. Gigi wanted to celebrate, and she insisted I sleep over at her house—something I was never allowed to do. When you suffer from REM sleep behavior disorder like me, you act out your dreams while you sleep, like totally, physically. The dreams can be wild, like you're being chased by wolves or have to fight your way out of a raging mob. You might punch the air or kick the bed. You might even get up and run down the hall at full force, not even waking when you fall down stairs and bash your head. But the cuts and bruises aren't the worst part. What truly sucks is that, because you're asleep, you don't know when it's happening, and your conscious mind has absolutely no control to stop it.

The best way I've found to deal with my disorder is to literally be tied to my bed while I sleep, which puts a damper on overnight social gatherings. The only friend whose house I've ever stayed at is Tessa, and my mom only agreed to that after two years of my best friend staying at our place and after long talks with Tessa's mom about how exactly I needed to be tied up while I slept.

Though I'd always managed to navigate this Mom-imposed exile well enough, truth be told, it added an extra challenge to holding my place in high school high society. I missed out on so much over the years, simply by not partaking in this most sacred of girl rituals. But tournament week had been amazing, and when I assisted Gigi in her game-winning goal, we were sisters, Venus and Serena, the best of ourselves because we had done what only we could have. Together. I didn't just want to hang out at a friend's house. I wanted to be with Gigi that night. There was no question that she was still the bride, but I was being offered an upgrade from bridesmaid to maid of honor. And I wanted to take it.

I hadn't physically enacted a dream in weeks, and I was on such an invincibility high that I convinced myself it would be okay to break the rules just this once. Tessa would be there to work my mattress restraints, so I'd be safe—we all would be. And for a while, we were.

Maybe it was the intoxication of the lie—my mother thought I was at Tessa's—or maybe it was the delicious taste of freedom, but when Gigi suggested we push past our tiredness and stay awake to streak across the football field's fifty-yard line at sunrise, I heard the warning bells go off and ignored them anyway.

I remember seeing the first hint of a blue-gray dawn and thinking I had made it. We'd been watching a marathon of some British show about teenagers with mutant powers and planned to sneak over to the football field right after the end of the final episode. But we must have all fallen asleep within seconds of each other, because when the unrestrained beast in me came to full, roaring life, no one was awake to see it. Not until it was too late and Gigi's life was literally in my hands.

When I'm in that state, dreaming, there are no social norms telling my brain to stop and consider what I'm doing. I act, and I react, and I do not stop until I've completed my task. I am all instinct, I am strong, and I am fast. What must it have been like for Amber and Tessa to see me, glassy-eyed and unresponsive but with Buffy-like reflexes? Surreal, I'm sure. But for Gigi, it must have been simply terrifying. She thought I was going to kill her, and had I stayed dreaming for one second longer, I might have.

As I look at Jamie sitting beside me, so faithful, so kind, I am tempted to believe his words. But I don't, because I know better.

"Thanks," I say. "You're a good friend. I mean it. But speaking of friends, I should get a move on, or Tessa'll have my head."

"Sure," he says, and he rises from the table, taking his half-eaten sandwiches with him.

"Thanks for upping my social status," I call after him.

"Anytime," he says. He looks at me for a moment, then adds, "For what it's worth, I think that cop just wanted to help Louise."

Tears prick my eyes, but I smile them away. I wave at him lightly, and then he's gone.

I stare down at my uneaten cream cheese bagel. This morning, during Tessa's get-out-of-bed-and-come-to-school pep talk, she tried to assure me that today was nothing in the grand scheme of things; that when I was ninety, it would seem like it only lasted a second. But after four periods of relentless cold shoulders, behind-my-back giggling, and to-my-face glares, all from people I once counted friends, I know she's full of it. I know, deep beneath my head-held-high, meet-their-eyes persona, that the memory of today will always make me want to puke.

I continue to stare at my food and scream silent commands at my sagging body. *Lift your head! Smile like everything is fine! Eat!* The words are as hollow as my stomach, but I'm nothing if not a team player, so I manage one action.

The bagel pushes past the barrier of my lips, and I bite off a piece. The cream cheese instantly turns to glue in my mouth, and the doughy bread is like a stopper in my throat. As my gag reflex starts to kick in, I panic. The only thing that could make today worse would be to vomit on myself in front of half the student body. I'm about to spit the bagel into a napkin when I hear it.

An explosion of cackling laughter erupts from Gigi's table. Are they laughing at me? Of course they are. I know—and have turned a blind eye to—the cruel side of Gigi MacDonald for a long time now. Yes, she could rally the troops to bake a cake for an injured teammate or arrange a girls'-only mani-pedi field trip for a friend who just got dumped. But just ask the *Horseman Gazette* editor who included a less than flattering photo of Gigi in the School Life spread, or the girl who gave mono to the guy that gave it to Gigi, and they'll tell you how nasty words and social media can cripple you. Sure, I may have suggested Gigi tone it down a bit in some cases, but if her withering stare was ever directed at me, I was always quick to shut up. As I've said, I've got enough on my plate to ever really consider rocking the boat. But now that I'm drowning?

My stomach turns again as the bagel absorbs all my breath. An image of her standing triumphantly over my fetal-positioned body flashes before me. And for a second, I think I might succumb, just like all her other victims that I so pathetically watched cower over the years and did nothing to help for fear of making myself a target.

But then I remind myself of what I just told Jamie: I'm not a lie-down-and-take-it kind of girl. So I do the only thing I can think of that might save me.

I grab the inside of my cheek between my teeth and bite down hard. The metallic taste of blood mingles with the gag-worthy food. It's horrible, but it's the kick in the butt I need. Closing my eyes, I swallow.

When I open them again, I catch the attention of a passing freshman, and I wink. He blushes and trips over his own feet, nearly spilling his little carton of milk. Some heat returns to my body, and I smile. Tightening my grip on the bagel, I rip off another bite.

I watch as Team Gigi exits the cafeteria. Though I feel a little better, I'm still smart enough to remain seated until I'm sure they've completely cleared out. I look at my watch. Five minutes until the end of the period. Tessa must be going nuclear in the hall. I gather my things and carry the remnants of my bagel to the garbage. It feels like a billion eyes are trained on me, but when I dump my trash and look around, there's only one person I notice.

I'm being watched from the shadows. Literally. Someone, a guy judging from his size, is staring at me from the far corner of the lunchroom. The fluorescent light above him is out, and he's too far away to see clearly, but he must be able to tell that I've spotted him. Yet he doesn't look away.

I run my fingers through my hair, loosening it so it falls in front of my face. I've been on display enough today. As I hurry out the cafeteria doors, I steal one final glance in his direction. He's still watching.

I'm outside and halfway down the hall in a matter of seconds. Yet I feel that gaze long after I'm out of sight.

chapter three

. . . .

W hen I exit the lunchroom, Tessa's at the far end of the hall, tapping her watch in anticipation of the period-ending bell. Though history is her worst subject, daydreaming about our teacher Mr. Riley happens to be her favorite pastime. No one, not even her very best friend, would be forgiven for making her late.

I'm halfway to Tessa when there's a sudden and terrible eclipse. Gigi, flanked by Amber and Kiara, a particularly tough teammate of ours who we don't usually hang out with, exits the girls' bathroom and plants herself directly in my path.

Gigi and I haven't actually spoken since the sleepover, despite the numerous pleading messages and apology texts I've sent. It's through Tessa that I've heard she's considering a restraining order and from my mother that I've learned of her parents' threat to press charges. Yet here she is, seeking me out. I just want to make this better, to tell her I'm so sorry, that I never, ever meant to hurt her. Maybe Jamie is right. Maybe she'll understand if only I can get her to listen. I push her bitchy gossip mongering out of my mind and smile.

"Hey, Gigi. Listen, I am so—" is all I manage to say before her right hand flies up and slaps me across the face.

I stand there, hand on cheek, mouth gaping in awkward disbelief.

Kiara glares at me, and Amber gasps.

Gigi grins. "You're welcome," she says.

Tessa rushes to my side. "Gigi, what the hell?"

"I'm just doing Sarah a favor, T," she replies with put-on innocence. "It's like that dog-training thing we learned about in Dr. Gordon's class. Before Sarah opens her mouth to apologize to me again, she'll remember that slap and think better of it." Gigi screws up her face and leans into me. "Don't you know karma's a bitch? I never want to hear another BS thing out of your lying, freak mouth, so long as I live. And I plan to live a long time, despite your best efforts, if for no reason other than to make your miserable existence that much more—hey!" she cries as Amber knocks her off-balance. "Did you forget to take your meds?"

"It wasn't my fault," Amber pleads, an incredulous terror scrunching her face. "That guy walked into me. Excuse me," she calls after him. "Didn't you see—"

Amber's words stick in her throat.

A tall, lean, but substantial guy turns to her with a playful, crooked smile. His existence seems as effortless as his perfectly relaxed jeans and unbuttoned flannel, but there's a definite hint of the Herculean straining against the fitted gray T-shirt he wears underneath.

Tessa raises her eyebrows as Gigi gives him the once-over.

While it's true that my savior is fine, I'm less concerned with his Adonis rating than I am with the realization that I know him from somewhere else.

My body stiffens. I grab Tessa's wrist. Though I'm sure she interprets this move as girly excitement over the hot new guy, to me, his looks mean squat. Though I've technically never met him before, this boy has already made a cameo in the black comedy that is my current life. His green eyes lock on mine, and for a moment, I think he recognizes me too. But how can he, when the only other time I've seen him is the night I tried to kill Gigi—in my dream?

Before I can even begin to process how the half-naked dream-guy by the tree is standing before me in real life, Gigi pounces.

"Hey, new boy," she purrs.

His gaze lingers on me for a moment more, and then he turns his attention to her. Gigi's not naturally gorgeous, as she'd be the first to tell you. According to her, her eyes are too small, too close together, she's got stringy, corn-husk hair that lies limp on her head, and her pale white skin borders on translucent. But what God didn't gift her, she's reclaimed through a preternatural ability to apply makeup and wield a curling iron. Gigi knows how to make the most of what she's got, and when she's finished working her magic, she's striking. Though the guy doesn't say a word as he looks her up and down, Gigi knows the kind of first impression she makes, and she's banking on her ability to use it to take me out.

"Since you clearly don't know better, I'll give you a pass this time," she says as she moves closer to him. "That girl behind me who you were just checking out? The one with the handprint on her face? You don't want to get too close to her. She's sick and highly contagious."

My dream guy's grin widens, and Amber giggles like a four-year-old. Tessa shoots her a you-and-me-behind-the-gym-at-recess look, and though I appreciate the effort, I know it's fruitless. Jamie is wrong. This thing with Gigi isn't going to blow over. I'm a marked woman, and even the new kid is going to fall in line.

"Contagious?" he asks. His smirking baritone transports me back to my dream, and I blush at the sense memory of his smooth, naked chest. "What's she got?"

Gigi glances back at me triumphantly. "Social leprosy," she snarks.

Amber and Kiara laugh. Tessa mouths at them to shut up.

The guy slides forward into Gigi's personal space, and for a second, I'm utterly terri0fied that he's going to kiss her. "So you're saying I'd be better off sharing a petri dish with you?" he asks.

"Maybe," Gigi says, sounding way less composed than she'd

probably like. She tilts her face up to his, and I want to leap between them and claw her eyes out.

He brings his mouth even closer to hers, and I'm paralyzed, imagining the heat of his breath against her lips.

Then, in a whisper, he says, "Unfortunately, I've already been inoculated against clichéd, high school mean girl. So I guess that makes us a no-go."

Amber makes a choking sound, and Kiara covers her mouth with both hands.

Gigi flushes blood red but doesn't move an inch, caught in an unexpected standoff with a guy who, moments ago, she was sure was hers for the taking.

It takes all my strength not to smile and incur any more of her wrath.

As the period-ending bell finally rings, Gigi snaps back to reality and steps back, effectively ending the stalemate.

"Interesting choice," she says, then turns to leave. She bodychecks me as she struts past, her two stooges scurrying behind.

I've been issued a reprieve, but I know it's only temporary.

By the time I regain my composure, my dream guy has taken off and is at the far end of the hall. Without breaking his stride, he glances over his shoulder and throws me a smile. Then he turns his back on the scene of his social suicide and carries on. I watch him until he disappears around a corner and wonder if he feels my eyes on him just like I felt his in the cafeteria.

"Um, what was that?" Tessa asks.

I shake my head, having forgotten for a moment that I'm not alone. "Well, Gigi slapped me, and we almost got into a girl fight—"

"Yeah, I caught that," she says impatiently. "I'm talking about him, Little Boy Lost on the Way to Homeroom. Yum. Order me one of those." She gives me a sly smile. "Unless, of course, you've already called dibs."

"What? No," I reply quickly, hoping my face isn't too red. "Do you seriously want to talk about some guy smiling at me? Because I'm still sort of thinking about getting slapped."

"Move on!" Tessa says. "That dude had your back just now. And unless you've been holding out on me, it doesn't seem like you know him."

I frown. I've already pushed the limits of best friendship with my wacky sleep disorder. How can I expect her to understand that I recognize this guy from my dream when it's completely inexplicable to me? "I don't," I say as I head down the hall toward class. *At least not in any remotely sane way*, I silently add.

Tessa claps her hands excitedly. "Well, maybe I can help with that. His name is Wes Nolan. Just transferred from some boarding school up north. Today's his first day."

Wes Nolan. I'm already scribbling his name across a thousand imagined notebooks, replacing the *a* with a bubbly heart. No. Too much, too fast. I refocus my attention on Tessa's detective work. "I suppose it's pointless to question your superior snooping?" I ask.

She cocks an eyebrow. "You know my sources are solid. I

overheard Principal Hatch talking to Mrs. Linkler about a new transfer student this morning. Seems your boyfriend's been in and out of a few boarding schools."

"Really?" I ask. I remind myself I don't actually know Wes and have no real reason to be surprised by this information.

"Don't judge," Tessa chides. She leans her head on my shoulder and grins up at me. "Bad boys can be fun. Maybe you should reach out to him. You make a great welcoming committee."

I playfully shove her away and continue toward class.

"Come on," she says, matching my stride. "There are worse things than having a tall, dark stranger come to your rescue."

"Yeah," I agree. "Like having one of your oldest friends make it her personal mission to destroy your life."

Tessa scoops up my hand in hers and squeezes it tight as we walk down the corridor. Having been my best friend since we bonded over hating naptime in nursery school, Tessa has never once wavered in her loyalty. We know everything about each other, like that Tessa's an excellent lock picker and has been reading her older sister's steamy diary for years, and that, when I hit double digits, I started having violent outbursts when I slept. While my other close friends, like Gigi, know the basic facts of my parasomnia, it's only Tessa who's bothered to learn how to secure the straps that keep me tied to my bed at night.

She shoulder-checks me. "Buck up, bub," she says brightly. "Things aren't all that bad."

I raise my eyebrows, curious how she's going to spin this one.

"If a kid who just started school has fallen under your spell enough to make an enemy of Gigi MacDonald on his first day, then you really have made an impact. I mean it, Sarah. This is way better than a sex tape!"

As Tessa prattles on, planning our high school domination, my mind wanders back to Wes. I can either freak out over the baffling coincidence that I imagined this kid the day before I met him in real, waking life, or I can focus on what's really important: adding that Puck-like, slanted smirk to the mental picture of him shirtless in the woods.

"He is kind of hot, isn't he?" I say.

"Who? Transfer boy?" Tessa laughs, thrilled to return to the subject. "Yeah. He looks as tasty as a banana fudge sundae with whipped cream and cherries on top. The question is, beyond the looks, is he anything to write a song about?"

"I don't know," I say coyly. "Maybe you should do some research, since you keep talking about how delicious he is."

"Uh-uh," Tessa replies, shaking her head. "That boy's only got eyes for you. Besides, I'm busy playing the naughty Lolita to Mr. Riley's Humbert Humbert."

"In your dreams," I snort.

She grins seductively. "Just a few more extra credit assignments and he's all mine."

We enter Mr. Riley's history III class and take our seats at the front of the room. As the rest of the students file in, Tessa turns to me, her lips pursed together. "I do hope he's not a total freak," she says.

"Who? Wes?"

She nods. "I hate it when hotness is wasted on the weird."
She perks up as our teacher takes his place at the front desk, her
concern for the ratio of attractive to odd forgotten. "Hi, Mr.
Riley. Nice jacket. Is that tweed?"

As Tessa flutters her lashes, I contemplate her assessment
of Wes. Yes, the guy is gorgeous, but his good looks can only
distract me for so long. Not only has this total stranger appeared
in my most recent violent dream, but then he shows up in the
flesh, wandering the halls of my high school. Did I see him on
the street or stand behind him at Starbucks? I wrack my brain,
trying to rationalize this most recent irrational event. But I just
can't shake the feeling that there's something different about
Wes Nolan. And no matter how attractive he is, in my personal
experience, rarely does different equal good. The thought makes
me twitch, and I have to put down my pencil before someone
notices. Though I'd have thought it impossible this morning,
Gigi's vendetta against me may have just slipped to the number
two spot on my *OMFG* list.

chapter four
....

"Welcome back, Sleeping Beauty," says a bald, doughy man with a '70s porno 'stache.

"What's shaking, Ralphie?" I ask. "Other than your belly."

"Hey," he replies, feigning offense. "I'll have you know I've lost five pounds in the last four months, Sarah. 'Course, I'd gained twenty since you were in the clinic last." Ralphie howls with laughter, and I giggle along with him; his joy is always infectious.

I met Ralphie at my first overnight observation at the Leigh-Erickson Center for Sleep Medicine when I was ten. Four months earlier, I had begun to exhibit strange nocturnal habits: screaming out in the middle of the night; kicking and punching anything near me (stuffed animal, concerned parent); falling out of bed at least three times a week; and even sleepwalking to another room and wreaking havoc on it.

My pediatrician and parents were clueless. My mother later confessed that they were actually considering an exorcism when she came across an ad that spared me. A nearby university had just opened a sleep clinic and was looking for patients to study. My mother believed this to be the answer to our prayers. But when I entered the sterile room with cold white tiles and a springy cot in the corner, I knew it was the beginning of a nightmare.

"I'm going to fill out some paperwork just down the hall while Mr. Berger here gets you set up," Mom had said that first night. "Everything will be fine." Then she left me alone with a large, strange man whose thin, upturned mustache suggested I was about to be tied to a train track. He wheeled in a big computer with what looked like a million little wires connected to tiny suction cups. I opened my mouth to scream.

"Wait, wait," said the mustachioed technician as he popped a few onto his own head and switched on the computer. "See? They don't hurt a bit." I watched closely as he adjusted knobs and fiddled with the keyboard. Then he sat on the bed next to me.

"I'm Ralphie," he said and held out his hand to shake mine. I didn't move. He smiled and asked, "How's about I make you a deal, Miss Reyes? If I can't keep you entertained with a story while I place these harmless little electrodes on you, you can scream as loud and as long as you want. Heck, I'll even join you."

I thought about this. "Tell me one for free, and then I'll decide."

"Ah, a smart customer," Ralphie said. He agreed to my terms and began the most magical version of Sleeping Beauty

I had ever heard. There were silly songs, limericks, and cameos by characters from other fairy tales, while animals and inanimate objects each spoke with a unique accent. By the time he finished, I was so enchanted that I agreed to the electrodes just so I could hear another story.

That night, hooked up to a collection of machines monitoring my brain, heart, muscles, eyes, and breath, I dreamt I was being chased down a beanstalk by one of Ralphie's German-accented giants. I had stolen a silver-plated shield, and escape was a matter of life and death. The video monitoring my room recorded me as I stood up and unsheathed an imaginary sword. I hacked away at the corner of my bed as if it was the base of the beanstalk. The next day, I had sore knuckles and a diagnosis: REM sleep behavior disorder, or RBD as us cool kids call it.

As the doctor explained my diagnosis to my mother, Ralphie laid it out for me in a way that I could understand. "Most people's bodies stay still when they're sleeping," he'd said. "They get a kind of paralysis when they dream. Not you. You can always move, and move you sure do, little lady. So whatever's going on in your dream, you act out with your arms and legs, your whole body, even though you're completely asleep. That's why you were a slayer last night," he added, trying to lighten the mood. Unfortunately, my mood was already way dark.

As Ralphie tells it, I was really quiet for a long time. Finally, I spoke. "I'd rather be Sleeping Beauty. Can we fix that?"

Though I roll my eyes whenever he tells the story, I'm always glad when Ralphie's assigned as my tech.

"So they got you doing this Dexid trial?" he asks. He parts my hair and applies clear, goopy gel to my scalp before placing the electrodes on top. "Thought you just said no to drugs."

"Let's say it's not a voluntary enrollment," I offer diplomatically.

As Ralphie well knows, I've had a couple of bad experiences on prescribed medication, and my mother put the kibosh on anything that messed with my blood chemistry, to the disappointment of my doctors. For the past year, it's been holistic therapies and nighttime restraints only.

"Who'd you try to kill?" Ralphie asks.

"Captain of my lacrosse team," I reply.

Ralphie stops what he's doing. I can't tell if he's more surprised by my answer or by the fact that his joke turned out to be right.

"Of course, in my dream, she was a wounded deer who I was trying to put out of its misery," I add, as if this will lighten the moment.

A look of pitying empathy shoots across Ralphie's face, but the pity is gone as quickly as it appears, and his jolly smile is once again restored. He snorts. "Bambi or Barbie—doesn't make much difference. You're still the villain."

The door to my room swings open, and an orderly named Barry drops off a tray with a small pitcher of water and a pill in a paper cup. An older man, a patient I remember from past clinic visits, waits in the hall. When he sees me, he points and raises his eyebrows, as if to say, "You too?" I shrug and nod.

When the door closes and Ralphie and I are once again alone, I ask, "Mr. Houston's in this trial? Isn't he a sleepwalker?"

"They're trying this drug on a bunch of different parasomnias," Ralphie explains. "Sleepwalking, night terrors. Not just what you got. Though RBD is the mother lode."

"Isn't it always." I sigh, allowing myself a nice self-indulgent exhale.

RBD is such a head trip. I've met grown men whose wives had left them because there was only so much of literally being kicked out of their beds these women could take. One guy I knew from an earlier clinic stay had to sleep with a helmet and babyproof the corners of every object in his apartment because he was prone to middle of the night ragers where he thrashed about like he was in a mosh pit. Another, who had a recurring dream about being a lion hunting with his pack, said he would circle his bed on all fours for over an hour before he'd finally pounce and tear the sheets with his hands and teeth. Not only was he completely worn out when he woke up, but there was little chance of getting past a first date with that.

Which is one of the most annoying things about my disorder. The disruption isn't just nocturnal. It affects all the waking parts of your life too. Especially relationships.

As if reading my mind, Ralphie says, "Hey, how's Prince Charming? You given him another chance yet?"

"He's great," I say, a bit too cheerily. Ralphie side-eyes me. I'm not getting let off the hook that easily. "Fine," I concede. "Jamie and I are *still* just friends, but he's mad at me. Thinks I'm being too hard on said Barbie for being an unforgiving shrew. Which is annoying, because he's probably right. I am the one who tried to kill her after all." I frown and look at my phone. "I should probably text him."

Ralphie hands me the paper cup with a raisin-size pill in it.

"This is the Dexid?" I ask.

He nods. Dexidnipam is the latest non-FDA-approved drug that the clinic is testing. In truth, I've been bugging my mother to let me try medication again for the past few months. Though she's been adamantly against it, I guess that when faced with either juvie or a patent-pending prescription, the latter doesn't look quite so terrible anymore.

Still, I have butterflies in my stomach. As eager as I am to move beyond the hypnosis and chanting and Mom's other homeopathic alternatives, I'm not a fool. There are always side effects, always risks. I stare at the little gold pill in the little white cup. Now or never.

"Down the rabbit hole," I say, and I knock it back with a glass of water. "Anything I should expect?"

"With the Dexid?" Ralphie pets his moustache. "Just a really deep sleep. One patient mentioned vivid dreams. He's having a recurring one about Grand Central. But that's all I've heard."

"So nothing to be worried about?" I ask with what I hope is cool nonchalance.

My tech smiles. "Want me to tell you a story before bed?"

I nod enthusiastically. Sure, I'm too old for stories, but even big girls sometimes need their security blankets. I snuggle onto the squeaky observation-room cot and pull the fraying, clinic-issued blanket over my chest. Ralphie fluffs the edges, keeping the blanket loose enough not to interfere with all the wires running off me. He sits beside me, and for a moment, I feel safe.

"Once upon a time," he begins, "There was a girl named Sarah. And she had a magic cell phone. One day, the magic cell phone said *Oy, mate—*"

"The phone is Australian?" I interrupt.

"What if it is?" he asks.

"Nothing. I just don't think of cell phones as Australian. American or Japanese, maybe. How about Norwegian? That could be—"

"Hey, who's telling this story?"

I smile apologetically.

He waves me away but goes on. "If it makes you feel better, the phone was adopted by a nice Australian family. Just be quiet and let me do the accent, okay?"

I zip my lips closed and throw away the key.

"As I was saying, one day, the magic *Australian* cell phone said, *Oy, mate. Text your prince g'day before he decides to put a shrimp on the Barbie.*" Ralphie wiggles his eyebrows saucily, jackhammering the dirty punch line of his awful joke. When I say nothing, he adds, "The end."

"Seriously?" I ask. "That's it?"

He nods.

"Ralphie, that was the worst story you've ever told," I say with a huff.

"Sometimes, bad stories have good lessons," he says. "At least the accent was all right. Besides, I gotta keep it brief. You'll be amazed at how quickly the Dexid kicks in." He does a final check of the machines and adds, "Just text the heartthrob. You'll feel better once you do."

Ralphie retreats from my room to the adjacent observation center where he'll monitor me all night long. It's a comfort knowing he's there, even when I'm annoyed with him for giving me good advice that I don't want to take. I stare at my phone, debating my next move.

"Trust me, kid," Ralphie's voice booms through an intercom. "The Dexid takes effect fast."

"But I don't feel remotely tired," I reply to the air.

"You will. So text him now or don't, but I'm making you turn off the phone in a minute."

"Okay, okay," I say as I give in.

Going to sleep now. Sorry about today, I text Jamie.

Good to hear from u, he replies immediately. Good luck and good dreams S. Sorry too.

I stare at his text, tears wetting my eyelashes. What's wrong with me? Despite all the crap in my life, I know I'm lucky to have someone as kind and solid as Jamie to care about me, especially after I've broken his heart and am being a total ass. I'm not sure if I deserve him, even as a friend, but I know I'm thankful for him.

I lift my finger to text him back, but my hand suddenly feels too heavy. My eyelids droop, and my breathing slows. I try to say something to Ralphie, but my jaw melts into goo. I hear a distant, echoing thud as my cell phone slips from my hand, landing somewhere beside me on the bed. I fight to push my eyelids open, but my eyes are already rolling into the back of my head.

Everything

goes

 black

 …

 and quiet

 …

 am I even breathing?

 …

 Then…

StingingWindFaceOnFire

 FlutFlutFlutterExplodingEardrums

  DryMouthCottonMouthSalivalessMouthChokingOnThe

  TasteOfNothingness

 UNTIL

blink—*A marble concourse.*

blink—*Gold lights.*

blink—*Stars in a green night sky.*

blink—*My eyes pop open, and I spring to my feet. I shake my body all over, relieved to have control of my limbs once more. I open my mouth to call for Ralphie but stop when my brain catches up to my eyes.*

I am not in Kansas anymore.

Standing at the top of a huge marble staircase, I see an enormous concourse with people passing through it below me. Arched windows, at least sixty feet high, surround me. A mural on the ceiling, bedazzled with stars from the night sky, hovers above. Below is a four-sided clock atop a circular information booth, and everywhere I look is another shining gold chandelier.

Grand Central Terminal. I've been here before, but not like this. Everything has a warm, honey glow to it. Veins of buttery bronze snake through the white marble, which stretches well beyond the staircase, covering the entire terminal floor. The tiny crystals that make up the acorn-shaped chandeliers shimmer softly, and the whole scene has a timeless, sepia tone to it. The lines of the staircase, the clock, the windows, even the people, are soft without being dull, subtly blurred, like a picture shot through gauze.

A parade of commuters glides across the floor in a grid-like formation, too choreographed to be real. "This is a dream," I say, and my body releases. My head grows heavy in my hand. Is it possible to fall asleep in a dream? Is this what the Dexid can offer? I breathe in, ready, finally, to rest. My eyelids are closing when I notice him.

He's running fast, a figure moving against the wave of commuters. He pushes through the people with little regard, but they're unfazed by the disruption and quickly resume course. The closer he gets, the more sharply he comes into focus. A jolt of energy surges through my body like a hit of caffeine, and I bolt upright.

Wes Nolan is coming right at me.

Bounding up the staircase, he leaps over a railing and lands at my feet. His green eyes are electric, sharp, awake. He is a techno beat raging against the three-quarter time of a waltz.

"Come with me," he says, and he holds out his hand.

I take it, and we run.

chapter five

· ·

S orry!" I call to a commuter that I've just elbowed as Wes pulls me
  through the valley of the dazed.

"Don't waste your time," he says over his shoulder. "It doesn't
bother them. They just reset onto their paths and keep going."

I glance back to see that he's right. The guy I hit floats back into
line, moving toward his destination, unaware of assault or assailant. As
Wes pulls me through the main concourse, I look up at the mural on the
ceiling. So many painted stars. It's night, isn't it? I am sleeping, dreaming. How funny to be so aware.

I move my fingers lightly over Wes's skin, its creamy ivory a
contrast to my own deep olive hue. I trace his cool softness, enjoying the
slightness of my hand in his. I blush and steal a look at my guide just
as he shoves another commuter out of our way. The pregnant woman
stumbles to the ground.

"Wes!" I say, and I pull my hand from his. I hurry over to the mother-to-be.

"Come on," he commands. "There's no time."

"Are you all right?" I ask the woman as I help her to her feet. She says nothing. "Hello?"

She doesn't respond. No words, no movement. I wave my hand in front of her face. Nothing. Then, without ever acknowledging me, she slips back into her line of commuters and drifts away.

"I told you not to bother," Wes says, the exasperation raising the pitch of his voice a whiny octave. "We have to keep moving."

I make myself heavy on the ground and fold my arms. "I heard you the first time," I say. "But I'm not much of a follower. I won't take another step until you tell me what's so important you trample pregnant women without flinching."

Ask a stupid question...

Wes's eyes flick past me, and his skin pales even more. "That," he says as he spins me around to face a nightmare.

Barreling through the assembly-line commuters are two hulking figures headed straight for us. From the neck down, they look like extreme body builders whose 'roid rage I wouldn't want to meet in a dark alley. Their bodies bulge and thicken wherever there's a muscle to exploit. If these boogeymen catch me, there will be no use putting up a fight. And yet their physiques scare me far less than their horrible, deformed faces: lips long and thin, pointing down in a sad-clown grimace; noses mashed and pulpy with crusty slits that at one time might have been nostrils. Their skin is pockmarked and craggy, and I imagine that, if I touch it, it will rub me raw.

But the eyes are the worst. In place of where they should be are two empty sockets, scabbed over with purple-bruised skin. If there is any truth to the cliché that the eyes are the windows of the soul, then these offer a view of violence, abuse, and infection.

I am too scared to move, too breathless to scream. But Wes yanks me out of my paralysis and pulls me to him.

"Can we run now?"

He doesn't wait for an answer.

We take off.

FastThroughZombieCommuters

DownStairsTwoAtATime

UnderArchwayOntoRampDownToTrack

Where...

A shining silver and red commuter train roars to life, and a bell chimes as the doors begin to close.

Wes sprints to the closest car and wedges himself between the closing doors, keeping them open just long enough for me to slip through. I am running fast, and I don't slow down. I fly through the doorway and slam against the wall opposite before collapsing onto the ground. Wes releases the doors and stumbles forward. Kneeling over me, he catches his breath.

"Not bad," he says with a smile.

I hoist myself up to sit and stare at the boy with whom I've just escaped something worse than Freddie Krueger and Jason Voorhees combined. "Not bad?" I ask. "I'd hate to see what's worse."

He lifts me to my feet as the train pulls out of the station. He leads me into the next car. Scattered throughout the compartment are the commuters I watched float across the concourse, sitting quietly now in their seats, staring ahead at nothing. We walk from one car to the next in silence. Occasionally, Wes looks back at me, as if to check that I am still here. I am. After what we just experienced, I'm sticking to him like glue.

About five cars in, I ask, "Where are we going?"

"Anywhere that's not where those things are," he says, more resigned than panicked. It's not that his tone is nonchalant, but neither is it terrified or desperate. Running from these creatures isn't new to him.

"What are they?" I ask.

"I wish I could tell you," he says with a shrug. "All I know is that when a Burner shows up, I run."

"Burner?"

He half laughs. "Like a burnout. I started calling them that after the first time one of them chased me onto a train. I hid in the conductor's booth and tried to calm myself down by saying it was a figment of my imagination, some speed-freak monster I'd created from watching too many B movies where normal kids turn into crater-faced hell beasts after one night of x-ing. Plus, their faces look like someone held them to a stove."

I shiver at the memory. "So, did it work?"

"Not at all," he laughs, fully this time, and his whole face lifts. He is so beautiful here, so firm, so defined against the fuzziness of my dream. "I spent most of the ride in the fetal position..." His brightness dims, and he trails off. "Anyway, the name stuck. All I know is, if I keep moving, I have a good chance of avoiding them."

"What happens if they catch you?" I ask.

"You don't want to find out. C'mon." He pulls me into the next car.

"You know, we're running out of train," I say. I can hear the

*irritation in my voice. Awake or asleep, I do not like being dismissed.
"Unless we pull into a station soon, I think we have a problem."*

*His eyes light up, and he stops. "Funny you should say that," he
says and points to a commuter getting to his feet.*

*He is an older man, white, late fifties. He'd be unremarkable in
a pair of simple striped pajamas were it not for two things. Unlike the
other commuters on the train, he sways slightly, a marked contrast to the
straight backs and orderly lines of his compatriots.*

Also, I recognize him. Mr. Houston, the sleepwalker from clinic.

*He moves to one of the closed automatic double doors and stands in
front of it, staring blankly ahead. It's as if he's waiting to get off at the
next stop, but the train isn't slowing. I open my mouth to say as much
when the doors slide open.*

*A gust of cool air shoots in as the train continues at full speed. Mr.
Houston wobbles on the edge of the doorway, and darkness whizzes by.
I feel the urge to grab him, to pull him back from the danger he's unaware
of, when what's on the other side of the doorway changes.*

*A series of disconnected images replace empty blackness until the
collage of bright colors and geometric shapes kaleidoscope into a portrait of
a park on a bright summer's day.*

No, not a portrait. A very real, three-dimensional world all its own.

*Though the train continues to move, what's on the other side of the
doorway remains fixed. If I were to step through the door, would I enter
this other world? As if in answer to my question, Mr. Houston does
exactly that. Stretching one foot over the threshold into the park, he is
about to touch down when I feel Wes move forward. What does he plan
to do? Save the guy? Go with him?*

Without thinking, I grab Wes and pull him back just as Mr. Houston's foot hits the grass.

His body is swallowed whole, enveloped by the scene.

The green and blue of the pastoral scene speeds away with the sleepwalker inside it.

And the train doors slam shut.

Wes yanks himself free of my grip and lunges at the door. He presses his face against the glass, but Mr. Houston and his world are long gone.

"What'd you do that for?" he demands. "That was our ticket off this train."

"What do you mean?" I ask. "He just got swallowed up—"

"Into a dream." He says each word slowly, the emphasis implying my stupidity. He stares out the window. "I told you we have to keep moving. You said it yourself—we're running out of train. If that happens before another dreamer opens a doorway out for us…"

A flickering in the shadows catches my eye, and I stop listening. I spin to find a monster with a spiked club arm standing in the doorway of the car behind us, staring us down.

Steam shoots out its mashed nostrils.

It grunts. It charges.

My feet move two steps forward on instinct, but my brain is so busy screaming that it forgets to tell my legs to follow. I trip and fall hard on the ground.

The Burner is instantly above me. He roars a hacking, congested battle cry that is all sour stench and radioactive heat. I scramble to make myself as small as possible, my intuition telling me not to touch the corroded beast. The next scream I hear is my own as my nightmare raises its spiked arm and prepares to bring it down on me.

Wes pulls me backward onto my feet just in time.

We turn and run.

We go from car to car until none are left, and we are trapped. "Help me," Wes commands, and he leads me to an automatic double door. We slip our fingers into the soft groove between the sliding doors, each grabbing an opposite panel to pull apart. We've barely moved them an inch when I feel a rush of air from the back of the car. Two Burners have arrived.

Panicking, I release my grip.

Wes is on me in an instant. Gently, he places his hands on my face, turning it up to meet his. "You can do this," he says. "We can do this together."

I don't know if it's the evenness of his voice or the steadiness of his hands, but I believe him. Though my hands are shaking, I shove them into the space between the doors again as Wes counts us down.

"Three, two, one."

I dig my heels into the floor and brace my lower back against the vestibule wall. With each micro movement of the door, I inch my fingers deeper into the frame until I get a firm grasp on the casement. I pull with all my strength, sweating, grunting, until, finally, the two panels give way, and the doors spring open.

On the other side is blackness. A night sky with no stars.

I turn to Wes just as a Burner appears. Before I can even consider my options, he throws himself between the monster and me.

I stumble backward, teetering on the edge of the doorway. The Burner grabs Wes, who is reaching for me, and I watch, useless, as his *arm vanishes, actually disintegrates, along with the rest of his body before I can grab hold. Then, a meaty, deformed claw swipes at the air in front of me, and I do the only thing I can.*

I go through the door.

Everything—

the train,

the monsters,

Wes—

falls away, and I am flying, floating, falling in the dark.

I know these falling dreams where you wake up just before you hit the ground. But what if there is no ground? Will I fall and fall and fall forever?

This dream is different, too real from the start. I shake. I hyperventilate. My pulse races. I have to calm down, but how?

When I was a little kid, before the RBD, back when a bad dream was just something that woke me up in the night, my mom would come into my room and kneel beside my bed. She'd tell me to think of someone I loved (at that time, it was either her or my teddy bear Mabel) and put them into my dream with me. Then she'd tell me to pick a different location and start a new adventure with my companion. Nine times out of ten, the nightmare would be gone, and I'd have a restful night. Of course, once my disorder took center stage, such childhood efforts seemed beside the point. Desperate times, however…

I close my eyes and think of Tessa.

My best friend, my rock. She always knows exactly how to help me take it all less seriously. She'd remind me it's only a dream, convince me it's just in my head. She'd make it all okay.

I picture her, laughing, running on the beach where she's a lifeguard in the summer. She's smiling, so I smile too. I begin to breathe more easily as I imagine that the air hitting my face is a warm summer breeze. The falling sensation is just like floating in the water.

It's going to be okay.

I'm going to be okay.

I open my eyes. Below me is a coral-blue hatch. I begin to accelerate. I hold out my hands and brace for impact as the door approaches.

Faster...

Faster...

Faster until—

The hatch flies open, and I fall through it. I land on a soft cushion of sandy beach. As I brush myself off, I see Tessa on a sand court, a volleyball pressed to her hip.

I watch from a distance as she flirts and plays doubles with a cute guy in board shorts. Though I glance over my shoulder more than once, no one comes looking for me, and after a while, I relax.

More or less.

Though she never sees me, I watch Tessa for the rest of the night.

* *

"Morning, Sleeping Beauty," Ralphie says as I rub my eyes. "You were seriously out, huh?"

I look down at my clinic bed and yawn. As Ralphie reviews printouts from the machines, Barry the orderly helps me sit up.

"What time is it?" I ask groggily.

"Six a.m.," Ralphie replies. "How'd you sleep last night? Vivid dreams?"

"The most," I say. I think of the running, the falling, the convulsing. "I can only imagine what I did in here." I blink my eyes into focus and search the room for evidence of a sleep-time tirade. But everything is intact.

"Well, that's the thing, kiddo," he says, beaming. "Your REM readings were off the charts, but your body didn't move an inch!" He grins goofily and slaps his knee. "You slept like a baby! How do you like that?"

This is the news I've been praying for for the past six years. So I smile and return his high five enthusiastically. But the truth is, I'm scared. The nightmare was so real, the monsters so alive.

"Is this a typical reaction?" I ask.

"You mean staying still at night? That's what the Dexid's for."

"What about the dreams?"

Ralphie thinks about this for a moment. "Well, I'm not supposed to really talk about it, but between you and me?"

I cross my heart and hold up two fingers in scout's honor.

"Remember how I told you about that patient who mentioned the dreams? You two are the only ones. That REM response is pretty atypical. Almost nobody else's brain goes like yours. Even your frontal lobe lights up!"

"Is that bad?" I ask, my eyes widening. "That sounds bad."

Ralphie laughs and shakes his head. "Not at all. Just interesting to a guy who looks at brain scans all night long. You're a dreamer, kid. You always have been, and no drug's going to change that. But dreaming's all it is."

Ralphie gets up and begins banging around the observation room, stacking printouts and fiddling with monitors. "Seriously, Sarah, this looks great! You've got a couple more nights of observation to make sure the Dexid's working right, and then, if we're lucky, you'll never have to see my ugly mug again." He pulls on his cheeks, jiggling them like Jell-O.

"I like your mug," I say. At least it has eyes.

Ralphie's right though. This is good. I should be positive about my results. I guess years of disappointment makes a girl cautious. But for once, I shouldn't look a gift horse in the mouth, and so I try not to.

After I've been de-machined and have washed the gel out of my hair, I gather my things and head outside to wait for my ride. The sky is a cloudless blue, and the light breeze feels chilly against my skin. Though I generally prefer the daytime, this particular morning fills me with unease. It's too bright, too perfect.

Like the calm before a raging storm.

chapter six

. . . .

"Now let's not make a habit of this," my mother says in her best serious grown-up voice. She winks as she hands me a folded piece of paper.

"Mom, when have you ever had to write me a note for being late other than on clinic days? Besides, if Ralphie's right, I could be nearing the end of my career as a sideshow attraction."

My mother frowns. "I'm still not sure about this, Sarah," she says. "I realize you had a good night last night, but I'm not convinced drugs are the way to go."

"And chanting is?" I ask with an eye roll.

"That's not fair." She pouts. "You gave up after two sessions with Dr. Ravi. I still think there are viable alternatives that could work if you'd just try them. I mean really try. Drugging yourself isn't always the best answer."

I glare at my mother. Though I have my own reservations about what last night's clinic experience entailed, hearing her articulate my unspoken anxiety infuriates me to no end.

"You're kidding, right?" I snap. "After six years of this nightmare, Dr. Erickson might finally have found a treatment that can give me a normal life, and you're telling me I'm taking the easy way out?"

My mother's eyes widen, and her hands shoot up in surrender. "Of course that's not what I'm saying, honey. I just remember the last drug you tried—"

"I do too," I interrupt, my temper escalating disproportionately with her every word. "I'm the one whose jaw locked instead of her body. And what about the time before? Remember how my hair fell out? Because I do. I'm the one it happened to. I'm the one that all this happens to. I finally made it through the night without moving a single muscle, so excuse me if I'd like to try being positive for once. I mean *really* try."

My mother recoils as I throw her words back at her, but I don't back down.

"This is the first hint I've ever had that I might be able to live my life like a normal person, that I might actually turn out to be something other than a total freak, and you're being completely unsupportive. Is this what they're teaching you in all your self-help workshops? If so, I'd ask for my money back."

My mother reaches for my arm, but I jerk it away. She places her hand in her lap and looks out the windshield at the sunny day. "You are not a freak," she says quietly.

Maybe not, but even I can tell I'm being a brat.

My mom and I sit silently in the car. I know it isn't just me who has been affected by my disorder. I doubt she's had a good night's sleep in years. Between doctor's bills, unsuccessful treatments, and my dad bailing on it all when I was twelve, my mother's suffered as much as I ever have. But she never makes me feel like I'm a burden, even though I know I am.

"Maybe I'm looking at this all wrong," she suddenly declares with fresh resolve. "Maybe there's a silver lining to this whole fiasco with Gigi and her parents. Maybe it *is* the Dexid." I turn to her, and she pulls off a smile. "I just get scared, honey. I'm sorry."

I drop my shoulders and say, "Me too." I lean across the driver's seat and give her a hug. "Sorry and scared," I whisper in her ear.

"I know you are," she says, her voice catching in her throat. "I wish this was happening to me and not you."

Despite my mother's annoying ability to turn an argument into a very special moment, my emotions get the better of me. Tears sting my eyes, and I laugh away a cry. "No, no!" I say, shaking my head. "I put mascara on this morning! We cannot sit here and weep."

My mother sniffles. "Well, we can't have you looking anything less than your best." She produces a tissue from her purse and hands it to me. "Don't worry. You look great, runny mascara or not."

"A natural beauty," I scoff.

"It's in the genes," she says as she flutters her lashes and fluffs her hair. "Unlike poor Gigi," she adds, her coquettishness turning lethal. "I'd forgotten how much work her mother's had done. In less than a decade, Gigi will be on Botox and her third nose."

"Mom!" I gasp. "What would your meditation circle say?"

"Oh, please," she says, shooing away my faux concern. "The second the MacDonalds threatened my baby, my circle became a ring of fire."

I give her a kiss on the cheek. "I've got to go," I say as I unlatch my seat belt. "Dr. Gordon hates it when I'm not there to stop Tessa from blowing up the chem lab. Thanks for the note, Mom. You're the best." I jump out of the car and wave as she drives off.

I face my school. The memory of yesterday's encounter with Gigi throbs beneath the phantom handprint on my left cheek. I think of the deformed monsters from last night's nightmare and wonder if they're more or less terrifying than whatever fresh hell Gigi has in store for me today. As I try to shake off the memory of the faceless beasts, I know my answer.

"Huh," I say aloud to no one but myself. "Something does scare me more than Gigi."

I laugh at the absurdity of my current existence and head for class. I decide to bypass the main entrance in favor of the lesser used West Gate, which is closer to the science labs. Though the security guards are supposed to lock all doors but the front after first period, they rarely do. But when I arrive, the door doesn't budge.

"Come on." I grunt as I rattle the knob. Still nothing. Feeling totally over the universe's insistence to screw me over in all ways big and small, I kick the door and call it a name that's far from ladylike.

"Easy there," says a voice behind me. "It's not the door's fault you're late."

I spin around, and my bag slips from my shoulder. I let it fall to the ground. Leaning against an empty bike rack, his long legs stretched in front of him, is Wes Nolan. His lips turn up in a half smile that forms a perfect triangle with his deep-set, shining green eyes. His sunny brown hair clumps in a chic bedhead shag, and aside from his perfectly imperfect, crooked nose, the only other technical blemish on his face is a tiny scar above his right eyebrow. But it can be forgiven, because it draws more attention to his eyes. And once you look into those, you're done for. If Wes wasn't so anti-high-school-hierarchy, he could totally run the place.

"Oh, hey," I say, steadying myself. "You startled me."

"Clearly," he says as his eyes bore into me. While Wes is an obvious descendant of the Emerald Isle, I'm one hundred percent U.S. melting pot—a hint of Latin America, a dash of Dutch colonialist, plus a generous helping of Southeast Asia. And while I definitely know how to put myself together, his stare makes me hyperaware of every little awkwardness. The subtle overbite that I sometimes pout to hide, the extra width to my nose that keeps it from being that perfect button plastic surgeons aim for. My face—and everything below it—heats up.

"What are you doing here?" I manage to croak out.

"I was waiting for you," he says, his voice sweet and low. He leans forward and narrows his eyes, his stare so penetrating, it feels indecent.

My lips part, and I take an audible breath. Electrical charges pulse throughout my midsection, and every little hair on my arms stands at attention. I try to swallow, but my mouth seems to have stopped producing saliva. I press my back against the door and feel the happy pain of a doorknob dig into my hip. Maybe it'll keep me from swooning like a nineteenth-century nitwit. Of course, if I did faint, would it be so terrible to have Wes break my fall?

"You were waiting for me?" I ask breathily.

"I wish," he says with a sneer, breaking the spell. "Alas, no. I didn't have a clue you'd be here."

I flush. "Of course," I say and look down at my feet in a vain attempt to cover my blushing face.

"But since you are, can I ask you a question?" He pops up onto his feet and is next to me in a stride and a half. He towers over me, and once again, I marvel at his physique.

"Sure," I answer, my voice mannishly deep, an overcompensation for the high-pitched squeal I fear will come out instead.

"I heard you tried to kill that cheerleader from the hallway yesterday. What'd she do? Steal your boyfriend or something?"

All the warm sensations cool.

"I'm sorry?" I ask, stunned.

"No need to apologize to me." He shrugs. "I'm not the one you tried to off."

"No," I say, flustered. "I wasn't apologizing to…I didn't try to…" I feel wet at the edges of my eyes. I scoop up my bag and turn to leave the West Gate. "I have to get to class," I manage to say somewhat audibly, but before I can put two steps between us, Wes slides up behind me. He puts his hand on my wrist, and I still.

"Wait," he says, his warm breath like kindling on my neck. "I'm sorry. I didn't mean to upset you. Sometimes, I speak before I think. Come here." He guides me back to the problematic door and places my right hand on the knob. Still behind me, he slides his other arm past my waist, wrapping himself around my body. He takes my free hand in his so that he completely envelops me. I keep my back ramrod straight, resisting the urge to cave into the shape of him.

"If you twist the knob with one hand while jiggling the exterior of the latch with the other, you can loosen the joint just enough"—the door clicks, and the knob releases into a full turn—"to open it."

Though the door moves, neither Wes nor I do. What am I doing, standing here wrapped in the embrace of this sort-of stranger? Just because I've invented a heroic dream version of him doesn't mean I know anything about him in waking life. And yet, all I want is to relax my body into his and see what might happen if I turn my face upward just the tiniest bit.

The bell rings, snapping me out of my reverie before I can find out. The hallway on the other side of the door will be flooded with students moving between classes in a moment. I should be one of them. So I extricate myself from Wes's embrace, nudge the door open with my hip, and take a step inside the building. But I don't go far.

"Thanks for the assist," I say, the squeaky girl voice clawing its way out.

"Not a problem," he replies, half smiling and not moving from the spot where I've just been standing against him. "I'm always happy to help a friend in need."

"Is that what we are?" I flirt, feeling a little more confident now that there's a bit of distance between us.

Wes considers this. "For now," he says, and his mouth grows into the wide smile I recognize from my dream.

I feel a bit woozy, and my senses momentarily falter. It's like that moment of total displacement when you're processing déjà vu and the whole world tilts a little before righting itself again.

"Perhaps we can get together, like friends do, and talk sometime."

"What would we talk about?" I ask.

"Sports. The weather. Your homicidal sleep tendencies." His voice is loud enough for the kids in the hall to hear.

I shoot back into the yard, letting the door close partway behind me.

"What the—shut up!" I hiss.

"Sorry. Kidding. I thought we were at the joking phase about that. But wait, is it supposed to be a secret? Because it was practically the focus of my peer orientation."

"Well, no," I stammer. "I just—"

"Not that I'm judging," he continues. "Based solely on my brief encounter with the vic yesterday, I'd say you were justified. But if you wanted to keep your RBD a secret, you probably shouldn't have tried to Elm Street your friend."

"I didn't Elm Street… Wait. How do you know about my disorder? And I mean, there was this deer, and it was hurt, and even though it was kind of violent, I was just trying to help it," I say, my jumbled excuses tumbling out pointlessly.

His smile disappears, and he grabs my wrist, hard. "What did you say?"

"Hey," I bark as I twist myself free, a clear-eyed defender replacing the bumbling girl of a moment before. "You don't touch me without a very clear invitation." Keeping my eyes on my potential attacker, I shove the door open with my foot and back inside the school hallway.

Wes's skin pales, and he stands stock-still, staring at me as though he's been scared straight.

Good, I think. I remind myself that he is, in fact, a complete stranger. "Whatever you think you know about me, *friend*, you don't. But I think I just figured out why you're such a loner."

Some of the blood returns to his cheeks. Though his body is still tense, he doesn't try to touch me again. "Why's that?" he asks.

"I'm pretty sure it's because you're a handsy dick." I turn away from him and head inside. "Thanks for your help," I call over my shoulder. "Hope the rest of your day totally blows." The door swings shut.

Stomping down the hallway, I spot Tessa outside the

chem lab, today's notes in hand. She holds them out for me as I approach. "I can't believe you missed today's lab," she says when I reach her. "It was the single most fascinating experiment we've ever done. I'm totally considering a career in the sciences now."

"That boring?" I ask, taking the papers. I determine to shake off my Wes encounter by focusing on Tessa's hatred of science.

"Listening to my mother talk about what's on sale at Stop & Shop is more scintillating."

The door to the classroom flies open, and a girl named Jenny comes running out. Her cheeks are wet and her eyes red. She clutches her textbook to her chest and runs for the girls' bathroom. Less than thirty seconds later, Amber emerges, smiling vapidly, without a care in the world, as Jenny's presumably ex-boyfriend Pete puts his arm around her shoulder.

"Oh yeah, that happened too." Tessa groans.

"When?" I ask.

"Last night. Pete's Amber's lab partner, and they were studying at his house. Bada bing bada boom. I guess he was tired of Jenny staying put at second base."

"What a creep," I say. "Poor Jenny. I didn't even know Amber liked Pete."

"Since when would that stop Amber?" Tessa asks as she claps her hands at Amber's turned back. "Hello! You discovered Proactiv and got your braces off three years ago! Ugly duckling complexes are so passé."

I laugh, rolling my eyes at my former friend's fatal flaw. We all have our thing. For me, it's the sleep stuff. For Amber, it's the memory of middle school. Before her acne cleared up and her head gear was removed, Amber spent every Friday, Saturday, and Sunday alone. She wasn't invited to parties, and she never hung out at the mall. But the summer before ninth grade, that all changed. Braces gone and acne cured, she was determined to become someone else in high school. But rather than discover that person on her own, she chose to model herself after the neighbor whose perfect existence she'd coveted for so long.

Lucky for her, Gigi MacDonald liked a project.

Gigi gave Amber a makeover and a lacrosse stick. And Amber proved to be a devoted and capable student, turning into a magnificent swan by Labor Day. But the price of Gigi's tutelage has proven to be high. Terrified of ever losing her spot in the limelight, Amber doesn't say boo without Gigi's approval, and she goes through popular boys like a mummy queen sucking their life force to stay young and beautiful forever.

I've caught glimpses of the empathetic soul inside Amber. Like when some boys from our rival high school were messing with Gillman Gilligan at a Horsemen game. The band geek had gotten lost on his way to the practice hall before he was supposed to take the field at halftime. Amber strutted up to Gillman, planted a big wet kiss on his lips (silencing the boys), and took his hand, leading him away from his tormentors. It was awesome and awe-inspiring. But when Gillman showed up at the Stump later that night in hopes of talking to Amber, her crippling insecurity won out, and her rejection of him was swift and fierce.

Like I said, we've all got our things.

"Stupid Pete." Tessa sighs. "What is he, JV center? She'll drop him for a varsity point guard in a week. See! Chemistry is totally dangerous. Why do I have to know it if I'm planning to be a gossip columnist?"

I glare at Amber and hope Jenny's friends know which bathroom to find her in. "You need it so you can understand the chemical reaction that causes nice guy A to dump nice girl B for social climber C, when she's clearly going to drop him the second something better comes along."

"That's not chemistry," Tessa explains. "That's Darwinism. But if you want to talk about that kind of chemistry, what's up with Sergeant Slacker checking you out from the other end of the hall?"

I look behind me. Sure enough, there's Wes, staring me down as if it was high noon and he's about to draw his pistol. A flock of freshmen girls moving en masse disrupts my sightline, and I strain to see through them. By the time they've moved on, Wes is gone too.

"I don't know," I say to Tessa. "I was locked out, and he helped me open the door. That's all."

"Hmmm," Tessa hums. "That's probably for the best."

"What is?" I ask, surprised not to get a sermon on the deliciousness of Wes Nolan.

"Well, after Dudley Dropout came to your rescue yesterday, I did a little more digging."

"Tessa," I chide.

"He's clearly curious about you, and I wasn't about to let my best friend get whisked away by a psycho."

"And?" I ask, despite myself.

"Looks like he might actually be a psycho. I nicked his folder from Linkler's desk during work study—don't judge," she says before I can voice my disapproval. "The last three schools he got kicked out of were for truancy, fighting, and, no joke, setting a fire in the equipment room."

"What?" I gape, though I still have no reason to be shocked. It's not like this guy and my dream Wes are one and the same. Still, the fact that the real Wes can't hold a candle to my subconscious's version of him is a bummer. "Well, that sucks," is the best I can articulate. "But there's no need to worry about me."

"No?" Tessa asks. "He's not the reason you missed chem? Good girl gone bad after just one encounter with Wes Nolan?"

"Har har," I say, waving her away. "No, just running late from clinic."

"Oh yeah! How'd it go?"

"Pretty good," I say, glad to think about something other than what a total bust the real Wes has turned out to be. "I mean, really good, I guess. Seems like they might have actually found a drug that will stop me from beating the crap out of myself and everyone else while I sleep."

Tessa stops dead in her tracks. "Oh my God, Sarah. Are you serious? That is amazing!" She throws her arms around me.

I smile. "Yeah," I say as I disentangle myself from her embrace. "It's good, I know. It's just…"

"Just what? Another side effect?" she asks, concerned.

"I don't know. Not exactly. I had this totally weird dream that sort of freaked me out last night, that's all. It was scary realistic."

Tessa asks, "Did you scratch your arms until they bled?"

"No."

"Did you run into your dresser and gash your forehead?"

"No."

"Did you break your boyfriend's nose or try to smother him with a pillow?"

"Not this time," I reply, grimacing.

"Then what on earth are you freaking out about?" she demands. She takes my hands in hers. "Sarah, be happy. This is great! You deserve good news for once."

"You know what?" I say with determination. "You're right. This is great."

Tessa links her arm through mine, and we continue down the hall to our next class. "Speaking of dreams," she says brightly. "I had the best one last night! It was summer; I was on the beach. I was playing...something. I can't remember what. Point is, the weather was so nice. I am totally jumping ship for the West Coast as soon we graduate. I am done with this New England bull—"

"Volleyball," I say quietly. "You were playing volleyball."

Tessa squints up at the ceiling. "Yeah, actually. I think I was. Which is so funny, because I'm not any good at it in real life. But, oh wait, I think there was this really cute guy playing against me."

As Tessa strains to remember the details of her dream, a chill runs through my body.

"Tessa," I say. "I think I had a really similar dream."

"That's strange," she replies absently. "We must've been talking about the beach yesterday. God, I wish it was summer. When is this stupid winter-spring hybrid going to end?"

I follow Tessa to class and don't say another word. Of course she's right. It's just a coincidence. Anything else would be impossible. Right? I try to focus on Señor Soloway's *lección de la biblioteca*, but it's no use. Between Tessa's dream and Wes's bodily embrace, my mental capacity is totally shot.

chapter seven

. . . .

"When are they going to make these wireless?" I ask as Ralphie hooks me up to the EEG machine. "It'd make tromping around the room when I'm asleep much less hazardous."

"Hey there," he scolds. "That's past. You're a Dexid girl now. No more sleepwalking."

"Sleep fighting, sleep screaming, sleep raging," I interject.

Ralphie ignores my embellishments and whistles a cheery tune. Nothing's going to get him down—or me if he has anything to say about it. In truth, I'm feeling a little giddy. Though I'm definitely not looking for a recurrence of my Burner nightmare, I wouldn't mind running into Wes again. The dream version, of course.

An orderly enters the room with my meds and a glass of water. He isn't exceptionally tall, but the way he carries himself—straight back, dropped shoulders, raised chin—catches my eye. His uniform of white jeans and matching polo accentuates his muscular body. The door swings shut behind him, and the sweet, familiar scent of clove wafts in. As he hands me my pill in a little paper cup, he brushes his floppy dark hair away from his eyes and smiles.

"Josh?" I say, recognizing the wearer of that long-forgotten cologne.

"Hey, Sarah," he replies shyly. He glances quickly at Ralphie, who's frowning at us.

"You two know each other?" Ralphie asks, folding his arms. I can already tell that the truth is the wrong answer.

"Sarah was a freshman when I was a senior," Josh says honestly. I wait to see how he plans to complete the rundown of our brief yet memorable past, but he says nothing more.

"What'd I tell you, Josh? You're supposed to flag the file if you know the patient off grounds," Ralphie scolds. "We'll switch you with Barry tonight, but if you can't follow protocol…"

"No, no. I can," Josh promises. "Come on, Ralph. You know I need this job. Mom'll kill me if I lose another one. I didn't think."

"You never do." Ralphie sighs. He looks simultaneously tense and defeated. "Rules are rules, and it doesn't just reflect badly on you if you don't follow them. I did this as a favor to your mother, but I can't have my job—"

"We really didn't know each other that well," I lie. "Josh probably didn't even realize who I was until he saw me in here."

Josh nods vigorously. "I didn't," he says. "I mean I knew her vaguely as a lax scrub back in the day, but really only by sight. That's why her name didn't mean anything to me."

Though I'm lying to get Ralphie out of whatever bind Josh's cock-up is clearly about to land him in, I'm not sure Josh needs to be quite so dismissive. It's true that we didn't spend a lot of time together, but the one night my freshman year that we did hang out resulted in my first kiss. Though the soccer stud was back with his on-again, off-again girlfriend by the following weekend (and, in more recent history, has become one of Gigi's occasional booty calls), I've always held that kiss as a good memory.

Ralphie eyes the two of us skeptically. Finally, he gestures to Josh and says, "Give her the Dexid, then go switch with Barry. And don't let this happen again." He turns to me and forces a smile. "Now let's have another good night, shall we, Miss Reyes?"

I beam back at him, probably overdoing my cheeriness, but I'm relieved that no one's getting into trouble on my account. "Yes, sir!"

As Josh hands me the little white cup with the Dexid, he mouths, "Thank you," and flashes a toothy white smile. My irritation with him vanishes. What is it about some guys that always makes you gooey? I tip my head.

I swallow the Dexid and lie down on the cot.

Ralphie watches us from the doorway. He holds the door open for Josh and shoots him a warning glance as the orderly hurries past, his cocksure posture replaced with stooped shoulders and a hanging head. When he's out of sight, Ralphie says,

"My sister's kid. He's had a rough time of it lately, but still. Total pain in the butt. He won't be in here again though. Sorry about that."

"It's okay," I say, yawning. I'm suddenly too exhausted to engage any further in Ralphie's family drama.

He smiles at me with genuine warmth. "Sweet dreams," he says and closes the door behind him.

Within seconds, I'm out.

. . . .

Flip. Flap. Flip. Flap.

I stand beneath the departure board, watching the flap panels flip over, revealing train destinations and time changes. I catch a flicker of movement against the uniform shuffle of the commuters.

Wes?

I turn, expectant, giddy with the sensation of butterflies doing acrobatics in my stomach. But it isn't my dream guy who's fallen out of line.

A short, pasty, ginger-haired guy in ankle-length khakis and a blue button-down sways among the commuters. Just like Mr. Houston the night before, it isn't a huge movement, and he never fully breaks rank, but he stands out. One of these kids is not like the others and all that.

But the closer I look, I realize I actually know him too. It's Grady Butchowski, genius little brother of Jamie's dumb jock of a best friend, the proudly self-nicknamed Meat. But while Mr. Houston's appearance last night made some sense—I'd just seen him at the clinic—I can't for the life of me think why Grady would be running around my subconscious.

So I follow him.

I follow Grady to track 32 and watch him stumble onto the third car of an idling passenger train. Though I'm curious to see where he's going, I don't jump on the train just yet. One final look for Wes.

The train revs its engine, and the trail of commuters wandering toward it begins to thin. I feel a tickle at the back of my mind.

I don't want to go without him.

I begin to sag into a full-body pout when the sound of quick footsteps straightens my spine. I turn just as a figure comes upon me. As he breezes by, Wes grabs my hand.

"Hey," he says and pulls me down the ramp.

I lace my fingers through his, and he tightens his grip. He glances back at me and smiles sweetly, shyly even. I squeeze his hand. He begins to lead me to the nearest car, but I pull back and say, "No, third."

He's surprised by my command, but his shrugging grin tells me it's not in a bad way. We hop onto the train, and the doors shut behind us. I lean against the glass partition that separates the vestibule from the rows of commuter seats. Wes's unblinking eyes smile at mine as he continues to hold my hand.

"Why the third car?" he asks.

"I recognized one of them." I point to Grady, who pitches to one side in his seat. "His name's Grady. Sophomore. Crazy smart. He's moving differently from everyone else, just like the man last night. Are they the only two you've ever seen do something like that?"

Before Wes can answer, Grady gets to his feet and stumbles forward. The sliding doors opposite him open, and he leans over the edge of empty blackness. Without a word between us, Wes and I flank him on either side. *Standing on the precipice of that same black hole that I had fallen into the night before, my heart thumps. I look across at Wes, whose own accelerated pulse twitches in the hollow of his cheek. He grins. If Wes is remotely afraid, I can't sense it.*

Suddenly…

A traveling carnival fills the doorframe.

Grady leans forward.

Wes and I do too.

We all take a step.

The cool air flutters against my face as I lean out of the train car. Though my eyes see cotton candy and Skee-Ball, I can hear only the wind and the chug of the train's engine. My right foot travels forward along with Grady's, leaving the cold steel of the train behind in search of solid, natural ground. The moment I find it…

FWAM!

The carnival world takes over. Organ music rings out through tinny speakers. The smell of freshly popped, butter-rich popcorn clogs my nostrils. Multicolored string lights that frame every game booth and concession stand flash in 2/4 time. My mouth waters in anticipation of the sticky, sugary awesomeness of the pink cotton candy twisting on itself just a few feet away.

I am fully inside the oversaturated carnival dream that appeared in the train door.

"Whoa."

I spin around to see where I've come from, but nothing is there. No train. No tracks. I glance over at Wes, and he seems as overstimulated as I am. He looks at me with those mischievous, sparkling eyes, and my heart rate manages to speed up even more. It's not just that he is beauti-ful in the glow of the garish carnival light. It's that he's with me; he's like me. It doesn't matter that he's a part of my subconscious, because I feel his presence fully. For once, I am not the only one. There is no difference between imagined and real. In this moment, I am finally not alone.

The only thing standing between us is Grady.

As I start toward my singular companion, past the teetering red-headed obstacle in my way, Grady loses his footing and angles sideways. Instinctively, I reach out to catch him.

And that's when things go really crazy.

chapter eight
....

Whoosh.

M y senses stop.

Silence.

Dry mouth.

Blindness.

The odorlessness of oxygen.

Then…

Pop.

All is quiet and dark. But it isn't the silent black void from my dreams. The carnival sounds have been replaced by the white noise of a fan on low. My eyes adjust to the darkness, and I take in the contents of the room I'm suddenly in.

I am seated at a desk. It's cluttered with textbooks and graph paper. There's a laptop and an unmarked orange prescription bottle. Just beyond the desk hangs a poster of Albert Einstein sticking out his tongue, and there's a standing lamp that doubles as a clothes horse, covered in button-down shirts and woolly sweaters. I turn my head to continue my survey of the room, but it's an effort, and to my surprise, after I look over my right shoulder, I have to take a break. But while my muscles are slow to respond, my eyes have free rein, and they dart around their field of vision, taking anything and everything in at warp speed. There's a bed just beside me, a closet next to that. Books are piled high on the floor. A half-moon shines through the window.

I push the chair backward to stand, but it's hard to control my legs. So I turn my face back to center instead and look down at the desk. That's when I see my hands.

My hands, but not mine.

I stare, transfixed, at the impossibility of what's before me.

My hands are literally not mine.

In my lap are two chunky palms with meaty fingers and fat knuckles. There's a writer's bump on the right ring finger, which wouldn't be the weirdest thing, except I'm left-handed. And then there's the dizzying fact that they're pasty white.

My hands, but not mine.

I want to hide them, shove them under my legs, and count to ten so that when I pull them back, hey presto, it'll be me again. But I don't, because it's also really...interest-ing. I focus my energy on the right pointer finger and wiggle it up and down. I can feel the tension against the palm—my palm?—as the ball of the digit lifts and lowers in its socket. I tilt my head forward to get a better look. But as my face closes in on the darkened computer screen, I freeze. My eyes widen as I catch sight of the impossible reflection that greets me.

Screw the hands. The face I'm staring at isn't mine.

Though all my senses are intact and my very own insane thoughts are furious and frantic in my head, I most certainly am not the person looking back from the computer screen. I lift one of the hands to the face I'm wearing. I feel its touch against my own skin, though neither are mine.

They belong to Grady.

Slowly, laboriously, I explore the rest of my host's visage. I am simultaneously a sculptor and his clay as I poke, squeeze, and mold this second skin. I trace the rim of Grady's glasses and marvel at the shift between sharp lines and blurred as I raise the lenses up and down. I pinch the skin above his cheekbone as hard as I can and can't believe how much it hurts. Running my tongue under his lips, I taste the furriness of unbrushed teeth. I open his mouth wide and close it again. I blink and blink and blink, but every time, it's Grady in my reflection.

This is the weirdest dream I've ever had. I giggle suddenly at the absurdity of it and hear an unfamiliar guffaw instead. I watch as *my* shock registers on *his* face. I am fascinated and frightened, anxious and awestruck. I lift my hand to his short, greasy hair and watch as it slips through my fingers with a speed and smoothness that I am unaccustomed to with my own thick locks.

And then there's the buzz. Every movement I make in his body takes effort and tingles. His skin hums, his muscles crackle. It's like static electricity emanates from the surface of his every pore. It reminds me of being a kid and rubbing a balloon on my head until my hair stood on end and my scalp fizzed. And yet, I no longer feel like I'm in a dream. This feels real-real, like I'm really inside Grady's room and actually inside Grady.

The thought sends a creeped-out shiver raging through me. A shiver that soon becomes a convulsion. I shake all over as Grady seizes. I want out, and it seems as though my host wants to get rid of me too. But the more I want to untether myself, the more claustrophobic I feel. It's like my whole self is caught in a Chinese finger trap, and the harder I pull against it, the tighter it gets.

My pulse—Grady's pulse—is racing. Completely out of my control now, his chest and arms are flailing, and his legs, though seated, are definitely not steady. I feel his knees buckle and his chest lurch as his body pitches forward. I see his computer keyboard and the edge of the desk just before I hit them straight on with the top of his forehead.

Howl.

Shriek.

Retch.

I shoot backward, like I've been trapped in a Jell-O mold and have suddenly broken free. I land hard on my butt. My hands touch down on soft grass, and the lights from the carousel swim into focus. The carnival music starts up slowly, then resumes normal speed, like switching from a 33 to a 45. I double over and collapse, sucking in air through my nose and pushing it out of my mouth, trying to regain control of my senses.

I feel a hand on my back, and I spin around to see Wes leaning over me. He pulls away, as if my movement has given him an electric shock. I push back to my knees. I'm on a grassy bank just beyond the perimeter of the carnival. Grady is nearby, lying on his back, blinking at the starless sky above.

I turn to Wes for answers, but before I can speak, I see them.

Three Burners headed right for us.

chapter nine

. . . .

We run to the bumper cars.

Laughing children butt their neighbors' vehicles over and over to everyone's delight. They don't seem to see us or our nightmare pursuers. As the kids scream joyfully, we jump onto the tarmac, weaving through cars barreling wildly into each other. I leap between two of them a split second before they can turn me into a pancake.

As I steal a quick glance over my shoulder to check how much distance we've put between us and the Burners, I'm distracted by a disturbing sight. One of the monsters approaches a family of three laughing away in their bumper car. As it gets closer, the laughter stops. The family—a mother, father, and little girl—sits frozen in their car, their faces blank. As the Burner shoves the car out of its way, the father goes flying. He hits the low fence surrounding the track and crumples to the ground. With no emotion, the mother and daughter pull themselves from the wreckage and *walk away. Then the other parents and children who are not directly in the Burners' path exit their cars and silently walk off too.*

Without realizing it, I've slowed to a light jog. I can't stop staring at the man in the corner. I know he isn't real, that none of this is. But I don't understand why no one is going to him. Why I'm not going to him. It isn't until Wes hollers, "Split up," that I force myself to turn away. Survive now, ask questions later. I have to get my head back into the game. I break into a sprint.

I veer toward the carousel as Wes runs for the carnival games. One Burner on my tail, two on his. I race around the perimeter of the ride, but like a satellite using the gravity of a moon, the Burner following me seems to pick up speed.

I jump the turnstile and leap onto the ride's spinning platform. The Burner is too thick, mentally and physically, to navigate the entrance. I allow myself a moment to catch my breath as the monster spins out of sight.

The dozens of lightbulbs that line the tent top canopy make the carousel unforgivingly bright. Once on, there's nowhere to hide. The piped-in organ music that's a half note off-key, coupled with the rise and fall of garishly painted horses and the delighted squeals from the carousel riders, overwhelm my senses.

When the cheering and laughter suddenly stop, I know the Burner has finally forced his way through the turnstile. I duck behind a yellow mare as people silently jump from the ride, mindlessly stumbling into one another as they move in an amoebic mass toward the exit. From my hiding spot, I count the number of fence posts between the exit and the entrance, knowing that the difference between getting off and getting caught is one hundred percent in the details. With each rotation, I watch the Burner barrel his way through the mob until he reaches the spinning platform and gracelessly crashes onto it. He is five painted ponies away from me. As he rages against gravity in an effort to get to his feet, I let the exit pass for a final time and count down the fence posts.

Four.

Three.

Two—

I leap off, landing hard on the asphalt. I've skinned my knee, but the sting barely registers. I get to my feet, jump the turnstile. Without looking back, I run.

I run away from the carnival, toward the dark expanse of tall grass that surrounds the fairgrounds.

I can hide.

I'll be safe.

I hear a howl from the game area. The Burner's battle cry sets my nervous system into spasm, and I stop where I stand. "Wes," I gasp, his name giving shape to my terrified breath. I pivot and loop around a corn dog vendor, gaining speed as I head once more into the breach.

By the time I reach the remnants of the beanbag toss, the area is deserted. The Burners have smashed their way through an entire row of game booths, leaving what looks like a natural disaster zone in their wake. I crouch low and move through the wreckage of splintered wood and decapitated Care Bears. A busted generator sparks at the far end of the aisle.

A particularly gnarly Burner with a jagged scar that crosses his face from left temple to right jowl is still rampaging through the hoop shot at the far end of the row, while his smaller but equally terrifying companion searches for Wes nearer to where I am. I catch sight of the smaller one's clawed club arm and lose my breath. It's the same monster that nearly shredded me on the train last night. Ducking behind the ruins of the roller bowler, I will myself not to shake.

The other one, now known in my psyche as Scarface, roars and shoulders his way through a half dozen basketball rims, tossing prizes and ticket stubs like confetti. When he comes up empty, I allow myself a moment of hope. Could Wes have escaped?

Just then, a pair of green eyes peers out from behind a wall of stuffed panda bears at the dime pitch. He is trapped between the raging Burners.

I can't will away the shaking this time. I want to run. And for a moment, I think I might. But I don't. I can't. I won't leave the boy who saved me last night. "Idiot," I whisper to myself as I grab three bottles from the ring toss and walk into the open air.

"Hey, Tiny!" I yell at the smaller Burner with the club arm.

I throw a bottle.

It shatters beside the monster, who growls and turns.

Wes peeks out from the dime pitch.

Our eyes lock.

I stop shaking.

I throw a second milk bottle and then a third as Tiny charges in my direction. With the Burners' focus on me, Wes makes his escape. He stumbles over a splintered plank but is up and running before the other monster, Scarface, can act.

"Funhouse," I holler as I turn and run.

I race past the Gravitron and the Tilt-A-Whirl, jump over picnic benches, and skirt concession stands. I silently thank Coach for all those afternoons of wind sprints, because Tiny can't keep up, and soon, I've lost him. But as I come around the corner by the Ferris wheel, I see that Wes isn't having as much luck. Scarface is right behind him. I am too far away to help, and my heart leaps as the monster swipes at Wes, barely missing the back of his shirt. I'm certain the next grab will be a success, but then Wes slips between two moving cars on the Ferris wheel. The Burner can't slow itself down enough to avoid the cars as they rotate directly into its path. The monster smashes into the ride and is leveled to the ground.

Wes and I reach the funhouse at the same time. His eyes blaze with excitement and fear and just a little bit of crazy, and I smile, because I know they reflect my own. He reaches his hand out and tucks a loose strand of hair behind my ear. His touch is electric.

God, I want to kiss him.

But a determined roar kills the moment, and Tiny emerges from behind the Tilt-A-Whirl.

We face the funhouse.

The façade is a series of comically disproportioned, grotesque caricatures. Curvaceous cartoon girls run from big-shoed clowns. Their trapped boyfriends pointlessly pound against mirages of themselves in an infinite maze of mirrors. Their flat-chested little sisters admire the illusion of double Ds in their warped reflections. And framing the doorway is the wide-open, sharp-toothed smile of a menacing clown.

Tiny's lumbering footsteps grow louder.

We go through the fanged door, into a corridor of twisted mirrors.

See Sarah and Wes, long and lean, flying down

the hallway, light on their toes, nimble as Jack.

Until…

See Sarah and Wes, stumpy and fat, wading through

mud, slower than the tortoise, won't ever catch the hare.

Our bodies take on the reality of our funhouse mirror reflections, speeding through the first set of mirrors, then slogging through the next. As our stunted figures push toward the finish line, I begin to doubt that our little legs will be able to sustain all this weight, feeling the heft of this illusion in every joint and every bone.

Then I hear an excited howl and look behind me at the herculean reflection of Tiny, charging toward us through the first set of mirrors at full speed. There's a door ahead of us, and I push with everything I've got against the morass.

As Wes and I finally reach it and break free of our reflections, Tiny lets out a frustrated wail. He has encountered the second set of mirrors, caught in the mire, squat and slow. He reaches for us with stumpy T. rex arms, but it's no use. He won't catch us here.

As we stumble through the doorway—our bodies back in our control—I allow myself a sigh of relief.

We enter an empty room with a tiled floor and a plush red theatre curtain at the far wall. It looks innocuous enough, but my first careless step smacks me back to unreality. The tile drops out from under me, and I plummet down to a subfloor. Wes lunges to catch me, but the tile beneath him falls away too, and he is thrown to the ground. I pull myself up and begin to crawl toward him when a blast of compressed air shoots up and hits me in the face.

I cough to catch my breath until the air jet stops, then I grab Wes's arm, and we crawl, over trap doors, air blasts, tilting, vibrating, and sticky floors, all the way to the red curtain on the other side.

Just as we reach our destination, Tiny enters the room, and he isn't alone. Scarface has joined him, and he leaps at us. His stride covers way more ground than either of ours, and he is halfway across the room in an instant.

But the moving floor has a dramatic effect on the Burners' already challenged coordination, felling both deformed giants in instantaneous and thunderous crashes to the ground. Tiny manages to crawl a few feet before he's hit with a blast of compressed air. He howls in terror and rips at his face. We reach the red curtain and abandon our pursuers without looking back.

We push through a series of heavy felt curtains, each one thicker than the one before, until all light is locked out, and we are feeling our way through dense, choking black.

I am lost.

I am alone.

I am searching, feeling my way in the nightmare dark.

Until…

Wes's hand finds mine. "I'm here," he says. "We're here." And I feel less alone than I have in years. We connect in darkness and pull and push until the curtain parts, and we are blinded by white light.

My eyes adjust to the main attraction, our final trial before escape. The maze of mirrors.

"Don't let go," Wes says.

Never.

Hands clasped, we go inside.

Instantly, I realize we've made a mistake.

The ground beneath us moves, and the maze turns like it's on a *lazy Susan. It swirls and spins, changing the way toward the exit with every rotation. My stomach clenches. Sweat tickles my hairline. I can't catch a breath, and I drop Wes's hand to clutch my chest.*

I spin around and head back where we came from. I'll find another way to escape the Burners, because this claustrophobic rattrap is not it. I'm nearly there when the open entrance spins away and is replaced with a mirrored wall. I turn back to Wes, but he's gone too. All I see is an infinity of Sarahs. I lean against my reflection and slide to the floor.

"Sarah," Wes calls. He is coming for me. Our hands reach for each other, but instead of his warm, affirming grip, I hit glass.

A roar thunders in the chamber outside, and I know it's just a matter of time before the Burner is in here with me. The mirage of Wes presses his hand against the glass, and his eyes lock on mine.

"Sarah, listen to me," he says in a voice that demands my attention. "No matter what happens, you will be all right. Just keep breathing, even after you think you can't. You will wake up in the morning." As he vaporizes before my eyes, he shouts it again. "You will wake up in the morning!"

I reach for the echo of him, but it vanishes, replaced by a meaty, deformed claw that clamps around my wrist.

Scarface yanks me to my feet so my face is level with what's left of his. Webbings of saliva stretch across the open hole that is his mouth as the rotting stench of his breath hits me like a wind machine. I try to turn away, but there's nowhere else to look as the monster envelops me.

All my senses shut down.

Like someone hit the mute and pause buttons on me at the same time.

Air pushes out of my lungs.

I try to take a breath, but there's no oxygen to inhale.

The weight on my chest is too great.

My eyes bulge until I'm sure they will burst from their sockets.

Every single muscle in my body tenses, and my skin prickles so hard, it burns.

Everything—

> *the fluorescent lights,*

>> *the mirrors,*

>>> *the Burner,*

>>>> *Wes—*

falls away until there is nothing left.

>>> *Maybe not even me.*

I am lost in this obliterating embrace.

. . . .

The first thing that returns is the steady beeping of the EEG machine. A perfume of antiseptic cleaner and rubbing alcohol burns the inside of my nose. My mouth tastes bitter and dry. My eyes are half-closed, but I make out gray grout around white tile that's beginning to crack.

The door to my clinic room opens, and light footsteps tiptoe in. I turn to see who's entered, but my head won't move, and my eyes won't fully open. I call out, but I can't hear my own voice. The air around me shifts, and I'm overcome by the familiar clove scent of Josh Mowrey. I try to raise my hand, to gesture to him, to tell him I need his help, but my fingers lie still. I kick my feet, but they don't so much as twitch. Even my eyes can't blink as my lids remain frozen at half-mast.

Through my half sight, I catch a glimpse of Josh leaning over me, and for a second, I think maybe my hand did move, and he knows I'm locked in here, trapped inside my own body.

I think, *Thank God for Josh, my friend, who's going to help.*

I think wrong.

Josh brings his face too close to mine. His smile turns predatory.

"You always smelled so good," he whispers as he leans his face down, buries his nose in my hair, and takes a deep, full breath.

chapter ten

· ·

O migod, stop. Stop!" A girl hisses. "What if she wakes up?"
    "I told you," Josh says as he raises my arm by the limp
wrist. "Dexid patients are total zombies." He releases my limb,
and the girl gasps. I note a distant, throbbing heaviness beside me
as my arm lands on the bed. Though my hearing and sight seem
intact, my body's totally frozen.

"No. Way!" the girl says, then she cackles. I hadn't recognized the whisper, but I'd know that evilly delighted laugh
anywhere. Gigi.

"So I can do anything to her, and she'll have no idea?" Gigi
asks. A metaphorical shiver runs down my paralyzed spine.

"So long as we don't leave any marks," Josh advises. He
presses a calloused finger beneath my chin and follows the curve
of my jaw down my throat to the hollow of my collarbone,

where he pauses and gently circles the exposed skin just above my chest.

I scream and thrash and punch and kick. But not a muscle moves. And not a single sound comes out.

"Ew, no! Perv," Gigi says. She slaps his hand away from me. "I've seen that Tarantino movie, and it doesn't end well for you." For a stupid, blind moment, I thank the gods for Gigi's presence. No matter what's transpired between us, it's somewhat comforting to know that she draws the line at sexual assault.

"*We* are not going to do anything to her," she continues. "I, on the other hand..."

A cool sweat sweeps across my body. Without another word, Gigi goes to work. I feel the occasional draft as my blankets are rearranged or my nightgown billows. I hear the faux click of a cell phone camera more times than I can count, accompanied by the occasional flash. At first, Josh offers supportive commentary, "Nice one!" or "Aw yeah!" but Gigi never replies. She has a job to do, and he soon quiets.

After some time—two minutes, twenty, a billion?—Josh becomes antsy. "Hurry up, Gigi. My uncle'll be back from his break soon. You've done enough." Apparently, her revenge is even gratuitous for the would-be rapist.

"Have I done enough?" She sighs theatrically. "Maybe just one more thing. A keepsake."

I sense her step away from my body. A moment later, metal clangs across the room.

"Hey, wait a second," Josh says. "You never said anything about this."

The panic may start as his, but it instantly becomes mine as an unseen hand shoves my head to the side and grabs a section of my hair at the nape of my neck.

Internally, I cry out. Externally, I lay there, dumb and defenseless, my jugular served up on a platter. Gigi twists the hair around her fist, pulling it taught from the roots, and in one swift motion—

Slice.

My head releases as her hold on me disappears, along with a chunk of my hair.

"Okay," she says with all the perkiness of a bubblegum cheerleader. "We can go now."

Josh scrambles to my side and covers the shorter section underneath with the hair that remains on top. He turns my head forward and props it slightly with a pillow. My half sight fixes on the cracked grout again as the smell of clove blows over me. Then the door opens, and Josh and Gigi walk out.

I don't know how long I spend locked in my body, unable to move, unable to scream. I'm suspended between utter panic that I'll never again feel my limbs or that Gigi will return for another (possibly literal) pound of flesh and yoga-breathing calm, chanting Dream Wes's last words to me like a mantra—*You will wake up in the morning.* Even if my frozen body would allow it, I'm not sure if I should laugh or cry that my only comfort comes from a figment of my imagination. The Dexid's frying my brain like those eggs on drugs, creating such real unrealities that some slightly insane part of me is beginning to wish the stuff with Wes and Grady was real and that *this* was the dream. Anything other than Gigi and Josh in my room. Anything not to be so terrified and alone.

Eventually, I start to feel tiny sensations in my fingers and toes. Then tingling in my thighs and across my shoulders. By the time Ralphie enters in the morning, I'm able to blink my eyes, and I've regained feeling in most of my body.

"Morning, Sleeping Beauty," he says as he holds out a cup of water. "How'd you sleep?"

I'm up on my feet and out of bed. I grab the water and gulp it down too fast. I double over as my body convulses in a coughing fit. My still sleepy legs cramp beneath the weight of what feels like a thousand pin and needle pricks. I collapse back onto my cot.

To say that Ralphie looks distressed is an understatement. But I honestly don't care. What is his empathetic discomfort compared to my tale of spontaneous paralysis, middle-of-the-night assault, and body-snatching dreams so real that I wonder if they've actually occurred?

My coughing fit dies down, and I open my mouth so that all the words can just tumble out, when the door to my room flies open, and a familiar, green-eyed boy dressed in plaid pajamas bursts in.

"This is my bed!" Wes Nolan hollers as he stumbles across the room and collapses onto me.

Before I can even twitch, his lips are at my ear. "Don't tell them anything. Not the paralysis, not the dreams," he whispers so only I can hear. "Meet me at the West Gate."

Even if I had the mental capacity to react, Ralphie's on top of Wes and pulling him away from me in a flash. "What the hell, Josh?" he bellows at his nephew standing in the doorway.

"He was already up when I opened the door, totally took me by surprise," Josh pleads. "He's delirious."

Ralphie shoves Wes into Josh. "Get him back to his room, and don't you dare let this happen again."

Josh shoots me a totally BS apologetic look that I would have spat back in his face less than thirty seconds ago, but now I just ignore. After Wes's whispered confession, I can do nothing but sit and watch, dumbfounded, as Josh ushers my literal dream guy into the hallway.

Ralphie kneels beside my bed.

"Sarah, I am so sorry," he says, his voice sounding far away. "I promise everything will be under control by the time you come in tonight."

I blink twice, then shift my gaze to my tech who, despite his sincerity, will most surely have nothing under control. Not by tonight. Not ever. How can he repair a world that's just fallen off its axis?

"I need to go," I say, my wits returning, my mind swimming. "I don't know if—"

I give him a look that must say I mean business, because he falls uncharacteristically silent. I stand, and he watches as I head

97

to the bathroom to shower and dress. When I look back at him, he smiles and says, "Okay, we'll debrief tonight. And I promise: no more patients barging in on your beauty rest!"

While Ralphie's attempt at joviality is a testament to his kindness, it only highlights how utterly insufficient he is. It's not that I'm just no longer in Kansas. The Emerald City has declared Technicolor war on my black-and-white life. And there's only one person to see—the wizard, who's waiting for me at the West Gate.

chapter eleven

· ·

The light drizzle that greets me as I leave the clinic gives way to thunderstorms and horizontal sheets of rain. Though I've made it to school on time this morning, the Quad is virtually empty. I pass a pair of girls huddled together under a Monet umbrella and clock a sprinter holding his backpack over his head. Other than them, no one's around to note my suspicious dismissal of the closer main entrance in favor of the West Gate.

Huddled inside the semiprotectiveness of a hooded parka, I jog around the perimeter of my school. As I round the science hall, my pulse quickens, and I pick up the pace, racing to the covered portico.

Wes is waiting for me.

I pull off my hood. I'm still dripping, streams of raindrops cascading down my face, but I don't wipe them away. Instead,

I hard-charge Wes, my finger jabbing the air that surrounds his chest. "What the hell is going on?" I blurt, my voice sharp and full of displaced anger.

He says nothing, just holds out his palm—and a folded piece of paper. I snatch it from him and read.

Ginger kid. Carnival dream. Chased by Burners through funhouse. Captured in maze of mirrors. Paralysis lockdown for at least two hours.

I look from the paper to Wes, my hands shaking.

"Same dream?" he asks steadily.

All the intensity in my voice dissipates, leaving only a whisper. "You were trapped between two Burners in the fair games."

"I was hiding—"

"In the dime pitch."

We watch each other, speechless, the beating rain on the roof only serving to highlight the silence. It's one thing to quietly wonder if your reality has turned on its head, but it's something else entirely to have your absurd suspicions confirmed. Suddenly, I'm tired. Exhausted. I slump against the building and slide down the damp concrete.

"Is it possible? Are we really sharing the same dream?" I ask, staring at the wet ground.

"Seems like it," he replies and squats beside me.

I sense his eyes heavy on me but can't bring myself to look up at his face. "You've known…"

"Since you mentioned Gigi and the deer."

His voice lacks any intonation that might give me a clue as to how he's handling this glitch in the matrix. I, on the other hand, feel exposed, barely stitched together by my skin. His poise feels like a direct challenge.

"And you didn't think it was a good idea to mention it then?" I glare up at him. "Maybe we could have told someone, stopped this from happening."

Wes shakes his head. "Told them what? That we're sharing the same consciousness when we sleep? That's sure to keep us out of the mental asylum."

"But the techs, the doctors."

"Will think we're nuts. And that's if we're lucky. If they actually did believe what we were saying?" He scoffs, the sound both cruel and condescending. "Best case scenario, they'd ask our parents' permission before they started experimenting on us." His hands clench in white-knuckled fists. "I, for one, am done with that."

Despite his height and prowess, Wes suddenly looks small. He takes a deep breath, shakes out his hands, and runs his palms across his forehead. Then he says, barely loud enough for me to hear over the rain, "I didn't say anything *because* I was afraid you'd tell."

He falls silent. It's a considered quiet, the kind you don't interrupt. So I wait. After a while, he looks at me and says, "I was eleven when I started acting out my dreams while I slept. My mother's super religious and couldn't handle life with the demon that was possessing her son. I'd smash all her plates at two in the morning or open all the windows in the middle of January because I dreamt I was a fireman evacuating a building. So my stepfather started sending me anywhere that would study me. By the time I was thirteen, I'd already been in a handful of studies at clinics across the country." He takes a deep breath before adding, "It was trial number five that sent me into a coma."

"What?" I gasp.

"Experimental drug called Sonambulum. I was unconscious for two hundred and seventy-eight days." He laughs humorlessly. "Ironically, my body didn't move once when I was in that coma, but I remember it."

"You were awake?" I ask.

He shakes his head. "Not exactly. Sometimes, I felt aware that people were around me, but I could never make contact with them. Never touch them or speak to them."

I think of the temporary locked-in syndrome I'd experienced the night before and shudder. "Was it like with the Burners?" I ask.

"No," he says definitively. "I'd take the Burners any day to this. At least I know that ends. The coma was just a void. I was alone, with only the occasional hint of other people around." His mouth tightens into a frown. "Do you know what it's like to be alone? I don't mean lonely but actually without anyone?"

I look down at the pavement.

"It sucks, like, for real," he says. "So when I woke up, I did everything I could to not be alone ever again. I tried to have a good relationship with my parents, to do well in school, whatever it took."

This part of the story I know all too well. Equilibrium is only ever tenuous for our kind. I regard the angsty loner before me and ask, "And how'd that work out for you?"

Wes smiles. "For about two months, I was okay. Then one night, I woke up standing over the stove, gas burners on high, flames out. One week later, I was enrolled in a boarding school that just happened to be a mile away from a sleep clinic where I'd get to spend the night whenever the doctors wanted."

"So all the schools you went to?"

"I'd get myself kicked out, hoping dear old stepdad would run out of trials to sign me up for. But he'd always find another school willing to take his money—and another clinic nearby."

"Wes, I am so sorry."

He winces. "I'm not looking for pity. I'm just trying to get you to understand why we can't tell anyone what's going on. I've been experimented on for a lot of my life. I lost the better part of a year because of some crap drug that never should have been given to anyone, let alone a kid, and I'm still being forced into trials. Now I've finally found a drug that works, and I've got no intention of losing out on it."

"Works?" I ask. "Last night, I was paralyzed after some crazy weird, really realistic stuff happened in my dream—a dream I shared with another person. I don't think I'd classify that as the definition of success."

Wes cocks an eyebrow. "Crazy weird bad or crazy weird not-actually-so-terrible?"

I stare at him. Is he really ignoring the insane revelation of our shared unconsciousness so he can flirt?

"I'll grant you the Burner part sucks," he continues. "But the rest?" He reaches his hand out to tuck a loose strand of hair behind my ear. I'm transported to our near kiss at the funhouse, and I blush. "Tell me it wasn't nice to have someone in your corner for once. To not be so utterly alone. Tell me we didn't have a good time."

"Maybe," I offer as I try and fail to suppress a smile. The wind picks up, and chilly rain sprays onto my face, providing the cold shower I need. "But this isn't normal," I declare. "We aren't meant to be in each other's dreams."

"Yeah, well, we aren't meant to be acting out our dreams when we sleep either. But we do." He positions himself in front of me and takes my hands in his. "I thought I was alone, Sarah. That no one in the world would ever understand what I was going through. But now there's you. There's two of us." His eyes flicker. "We were made different, and we've been punished for it our whole lives, haven't we? How old were you the first time you physically hurt your parents after you crawled into their bed? How long did it take to figure out they were actually afraid of you?"

His light touch hardens, and he twists my wrists to face up. "When did you start applying makeup to cover the bruises that your restraints left behind? Did you hate summer and short sleeves? Were you relieved every October when your sweatshirts could help you hide the truth?"

I pull my hands back and massage them, trying to rub out the memory we clearly share.

"I don't mean to upset you," he says, his voice tight, a forced calm. "I just want you to really think this through. I mean, what if you actually embraced the Dexid? What if you allowed the positive to outweigh the negative? You've earned that choice, haven't you? I think I have. I think we both have."

"But *does* it work?" I ask again. "I'm not trying to be difficult, Wes. I mean, yeah, we've been through a lot and finally—"

"Finally, our bodies are staying still through the night," he interrupts.

"Yes, but at what cost?" I think of Gigi's middle-of-the-night visit for the first time since Wes and I began our dream deconstruction, and my hand goes to the shorter patch of hair hidden underneath. To be that vulnerable, to have no way to protect my sleeping body. Is this an acceptable risk? I prepare to tell him about the nightmare he didn't witness, but his temper turns out to be quicker than my confession.

"Jesus, Sarah," he snaps. He pushes back on his heels and crosses his arms. "Nothing's perfect, but isn't this close? Yeah, you might have some messed-up dreams, but they're not reality. Reality is your body won't freak out while you sleep. Don't you understand? This is the best we're ever going to get." He eyes me through narrowed slits. "Or maybe I've got you all wrong. Maybe things haven't been as tough on you as I'd assumed."

A tingling fury explodes across my body. It's one thing to listen to him bemoan his inarguably crappy childhood, but I'll be damned if Wes is going to accuse mine of being perfect. "I get that the Dexid stills our bodies," I say. "And believe me, that is not something I'd trade lightly. But it also puts your brain in mine or the other way around or something else totally nuts, and that is way screwed up! Not to mention there are monsters— *monsters*—that paralyze us if they catch us. So you ask what I want? I just want to be normal! That's all I've ever wanted. Isn't that what you want?"

"No," he says. "I want you."

Like that, my anger evaporates, and I pray I don't burn from the heat consuming my flesh.

"I've always been on my own," he says. "Not just in the coma, but always, everywhere. Until you showed up at the clearing in the woods. You found me, Sarah. For the first time, I was not alone."

This time, Wes blushes. "I gave up on normal a long time ago. I'll take the company and be happy for it. The Burner thing sucks, royally. And I don't know what to do other than get better at dodging them or look for a way to get rid of them. But that one minus, big as it is, feels like nothing compared to all the fascinating stuff that comes with this." He moves closer again, returning to my personal space, and rests his hands on the cool pavement on either side of my legs. His dazzling green eyes sparkle even in the gray absence of sunshine. "So let's keep it to ourselves. At least for a little while. This could be the adventure of our lives."

He lowers his forehead until it meets mine. Leaning on me, as if for support, this strong, brave, larger-than-life person who's taken up my plight against Gigi, who's guided me through our impossibly shared unconsciousness, closes his eyes and whispers, "Please."

I breathe him in. Wes's vulnerability makes me feel strong, despite my fears. Maybe he's right. What's a fleeting nightmare in exchange for the freedom of a consequence-free consciousness? Could I handle a brief lock-up for a life sentence of peaceful sleep?

"I want to," I say, matching the intimate whisper of his plea. "But I'm scared."

"I'll protect you," he says.

I feel the heat of his breath on my lips as his mouth moves closer to mine, and I'm lost, desire replacing fear almost completely. I open my mouth to swallow his, when the sound of a toppling garbage can kills the moment.

"Uhhh, whoops. Sorry," a clipped, nasal voice says.

Wes and I break away instantly, as if we've been caught doing something way more intimate. I smooth my hair as he adjusts his jacket.

"Hey, Sarah and guy who isn't Jamie," a runty red head says.

"Grady," I reply, rolling my eyes and waving Meat Butchowski's little brother away like a gnat.

Then the world stops for the second time that morning. The dream from the night before hits me like a sucker punch. The train, the carnival, the bedroom, the computer.

The computer. Grady's reflection in the computer.

I lurch at Grady, grabbing him by the arm, and twist him to face me.

"Easy there," he says, pulling his arm back. "Seems like you're already spoken for." His free hand adjusts his glasses, which are taped together at the bridge. A decent-size bandage covers his left temple.

"What happened to your head?" I ask.

Grady frowns. "Let's just say I was testing out a new product and had a close encounter with the edge of my desk."

My stomach falls into my feet. Grady is a straight-A student, a member of Mensa, and a drug kingpin. Unlike his brother, Grady can't expect an athletic scholarship to college, so he came up with a different way to ensure he could afford the Ivy of his choice. Tessa heard that he chooses which drugs to sell to whom based on the side effects. He likes selling Meat anything with hair loss in the fine print, while a hot girl looking to get high is guaranteed the added benefit of an increased sex drive. But to whom do you sell the drug with a side effect of possession?

"What new product?" I demand.

Grady grins. "I thought you were on the straight and narrow, Miss Reyes." He glances over at Wes. "Guess I had you pegged wrong. But listen, if you're really interested, I wouldn't start out with this stuff. A little too potent for a newbie such as yourself. I'd suggest something more—"

"What's the drug, Grady?" I ask again, my impatience straining my voice.

He shrugs, enjoying his bit of power. "It's not on the street yet. I really can't say."

"Tell her," Wes growls and moves to tower over the smaller boy.

Determining that an ass-kicking isn't worth the cover-up, Grady spills. "It's called Dexidnipam," he says with a sigh. "But I don't plan on selling it. The guy I got it from didn't own up to the fact that it's not FDA-approved yet, so the side effects aren't all in. And judging from my not so little fall," he says, wincing as he touches his forehead, "I'd say there are some serious kinks in the system."

"Who gave it to you?" I ask.

"Now, Sarah, as I've said, this really isn't the high for you. If you want me to sell you something, you're going to have to let me recommend it."

"Who?" I roar as I dig my nails into my own scalp and tug on my hair.

For the first time, Grady looks legitimately nervous. I watch him weigh the pros and cons of revealing his source to this clearly unhinged lunatic. "Fine," he says finally. "It's not like I'll be doing business with him again. You probably know him too. He went here. Do you remember Josh Mowrey?"

Without a word, I turn from Grady and Wes and walk away.

chapter twelve

. . . .

Using Wes's jiggle and jerk technique, I throw open the door to the school hallway and march inside. The bell for homeroom rings, and soon, I'm swimming upstream against wave after wave of my classmates. Wes catches up to me and walks silently at my side. Though I'm not ready to talk to him, his secret service–esque presence feels like the only thing standing between me and a total mental meltdown.

He keeps pace, following me wherever I lead. Thing is, I have no specific destination. I just want to lose myself in the sea of students surrounding me. But instead of blending into the masses, I feel totally on display, like I'm wearing a scarlet letter that reveals all my secrets and condemns me for them. Is it paranoia, or is every third person I pass looking at me? My chest tightens as my heartbeat jackhammers. Only this time, I've trapped myself.

Is there any way out of this madness? After a while of aimless wandering, Wes pulls me into an empty classroom.

"Tell me what happened in the dream with Grady," he demands once we're alone.

I've thought of a half dozen rationalizations for what I experienced, but I know every one of them is wrong. Finally, I say the only thing I'm sure is true. "I fell into him."

Wes doesn't run screaming. Instead, he says, "That's pretty much exactly what it looked like to me. When you went to catch him, both your bodies went into spasm. It didn't last long. The seizure was over before I could even reach out to you. But when it stopped, you two were, well, linked. Your body"—he searches for the right word—"*attached* to his. It sounds crazy, I know, but it looked like you were suctioned to him."

"What doesn't sound crazy?" I say. I know exactly what he means. "Except it wasn't like an embrace."

"No," he agrees. "Your body outlined his, from head to toe, hand to hand."

"Like Peter Pan's shadow."

"Exactly," he says with an excitement that makes me queasy. "What did it feel like?"

"I didn't feel as though any part of me was separate from him at all," I answer, just letting the words come. "I was inside him. But I wasn't in the dream anymore. I was in his room. Wes," I say. I look at him desperately. "I was in control."

The boy who's been unflappable until now jerks back.

"What? What do you mean? You could move him? Like, his real body? In his actual room?"

"Yes," I say with confidence. I passed incomprehensible one possession and two shared dreams ago. Why deny the facts anymore? "I wasn't very good at it. It took a lot of concentration to move him, and in the end, he had a seizure or something, and I was thrown out of him, back into the dream."

Wes is silent. It's my turn to leave him speechless now.

"This is because of the Dexid too, isn't it?" I state more than ask.

He nods. "It has to be. I was on it. You were on it. And we now know Grady was on it too. Just think of when we first saw him in the station. He was different from the other commuters. He looked buzzed, weaving in and out of his line."

"Like Mr. Houston from the night before," I add, an imagined lightbulb turning on above my head.

"Who?"

"The old guy you wanted to follow off the train the first night I was on Dexid. I recognized him from the clinic. He's in the same trial as we are. So he was on the Dexid too." I frown. "But he didn't react like we did. He looked more like Grady."

"Does he have RBD?"

I shake my head. "Sleepwalker."

"Then that's got to be it," Wes says, his nodding picking up speed. "The old guy isn't like us. He's like Grady, like any regular person. Something about the Dexid makes anyone taking it able to interact while we're asleep. But while their reaction to the Dexid is passive and they can be possessed, ours puts us in the driver's seat." Wes whistles as he sits back on a desk. "Holy shit, Sarah. Do you know what this means?"

"Yeah," I say and throw open the door. "Totally not normal."

I push my way back into the hallway horde, ducking my head as I start for my locker. I walk fast, weaving through the kids surrounding me, barely registering it when I sideswipe a book bag or ricochet off a water fountain. Wes catches up to me as the crowds thin and my classmates enter their homerooms for roll call. I don't stop moving.

As we near my locker, student council VP Trisha Goldmark begins the daily announcements over the school's PA system. I'm not paying much attention to what she's saying, absorbed as I am in the revelations of the morning (and it isn't even nine o'clock). Still, it's impossible to totally ignore her super peppy delivery, which is only one of the reasons why I notice when she hands the mic to someone else.

"Thanks, Trisha," Gigi says. My stomach flips. "I know I'm supposed to do the athletic announcements this morning, but there's something more important I need to talk to our class-mates about." Her voice breaks, and she takes a moment to clear her throat. "There is a dangerous predator among us," she says with resolve. "And she needs to be put away. I was her first victim, so some might say I'm biased. But you don't have to take my word for it. Take hers."

Suddenly, Gigi's voice is replaced with mine.

"I'm a freak. A nightmare," a prerecorded version of me says.

I sound small, whimpering, pathetic. "I should be chained up for what I did to you. At all times—not just at night. I don't know what's wrong with me. No one does." A choked sob reverberates off the metal-lockered walls. "They've never been able to figure it out. They probably never will. I'm a monster. I don't deserve your forgiveness, and I don't expect it. I deserve horrible things. Horrible, horrible—"

The recording of me shuts off, and the shuffling of bodies can be heard over the loudspeaker. It's followed by a sharp burst of feedback. Then silence.

I teeter slightly and reach out my hand to steady myself against the wall. Wes catches me. I feel his body, taught and strong, a pillar. I accept his strength, but I can't look at him. This is simply too much. Not only am I the star of some supernatural teen drama, but the boy I'm either infected with or crushing on (or both) has just heard the moment I hit rock bottom.

The recording is the final voice mail I left for Gigi after the slumber party. I remember crying that night, not only because of what I was and what I'd done, but also because I'd been rejected by someone who I so wanted to understand me. No matter how much I intellectually understood her well-earned stance, it had been devastating to realize I was not going to be forgiven. If only I'd known how much worse things would get.

"Thanks," I manage as I force myself to take one step, then another, and continue, head bent, down the hallway. As I turn the corner, my focus is firmly on my feet, which is why I don't see what's happening at my locker until I'm almost in front of it.

Tessa's there, ripping little pieces of paper off the cold gray metal, grunting as she swipes at a large object stuck to the locker door. When she sees me, she stops and runs toward me, desperate to turn my body away. "Sarah, let's just leave. There's no reason to go over there."

I push her aside and look. Though I've no doubt she's made a valiant effort to spare me the cruelty that awaits, Tessa's barely made a dent in the collage of incriminating photos that creates a mosaic wreath around my locker. The pictures are the ones Gigi took of me at the sleep clinic: vegetative, covered in electrodes, hair gooped in gel. I feel sick. But the nausea isn't just because of the photos. It's also due to seeing myself, hung in effigy at the center of the circle.

Glued to my locker is a doll's four-poster bed, pink and frilly. A Barbie lies atop the covers, her arms and legs spread wide, each one chained to one of the four posts of the bed. Her doll hair has been cut off, and in its place is dark human hair, glued to the plastic doll scalp. I can't stop my hand from reaching for where that same dark hair was once attached to my own head. Out of the corner of my eye, I see Wes watching me. He lifts his hand to his mouth and closes it in a tight fist as he understands.

He walks to the locker and rips the toy bed off in a single strongman move. Tessa resumes ripping the pictures down. I just stare, watching them as they work, though not really seeing at all.

The sound of a text alert on my cell brings me back. Tessa's phone has buzzed too, and, true to form, she's on her screen before I've even pulled my phone from my pocket.

"Sarah, don't..." is all I hear her say before my eyes fix on my own screen and one of Gigi's photos of me from the clinic.

Two girls exit a nearby bathroom, laughing about something on their cells. One of them is Kiara. When she sees me, her face lights up. She lifts her phone, points, and clicks. Tessa's on her in a flash, demanding she delete the photo and generally reading her the riot act, but Kiara ignores her. That's when I realize the picture wasn't just texted to me but to the entire IHS student body.

Wes, who's finished disposing of the photos, stands beside me. He asks, "Now have you suffered enough?"

I look directly at him for the first time since we left the class-room. If its pity or maudlin empathy I fear seeing, I needn't have worried. His eyes are hard. Though it's been at most ten minutes since our conversation at the West Gate, it's been a rather event-ful period of time. "You saw Grady's forehead?" I ask.

"I did," he says.

"And you think I was really in him? In control of his body?"

He nods.

"Because we were both on Dexid? That you and I can actually control people if they're on it too?"

"Yes."

I swallow, figuratively choking down my hesitations and fears, before asking the question that I know will change every-thing. "Do you think we can do it again?"

The hint of a smile twists the corners of Wes's mouth. "I do," he says. Then he adds, "And if we double the dose, we might have better control than you did with Grady, maybe even be able to stay inside longer before seizing out. So get two pills tonight."

"Sure," I say absently, my mind working hard to process so many things. "But how do we get…" I take a deep breath before saying her name. "How do we get Gigi to take the Dexid?"

Wes puts his hand on my cheek and looks at me. My darting eyes come to rest on his.

"I'll handle it," he says. His voice is soft, comforting. You'd never know he just offered to drug a girl so I could mess her up.

"Then I'll see you at the train station tonight."

I turn, not waiting for a reply. I walk down the hall and out of the building before I can second-guess this choice.

That night at the clinic, I'm quiet as Ralphie hooks me up. I fake dropping the first Dexid pill so he'll get me another. Then I down both in one quick gulp. When I open my eyes in Grand Central, Wes is waiting for me, and a sleeping, Dexid-dosed Gigi sways along the platform of track 29.

As I follow her onto the train, I acknowledge to myself that there's a line, I'm about to cross it, and I'm cool with that. Besides, I may be a vengeful, dream-invading, puppet-master head case, but for the first time ever, I'm not alone.

chapter thirteen

*P*asta. She's making pasta?" Wes slumps against the polished granite countertop of the HGTV-approved, Stepford kitchen, looking totally over it. Who can blame him? Here we are, brimming with rage, prepped for vengeance, expecting nothing less than Thunderdome, and Gigi's dream is a total yawn.

"At least Grady had the good manners to give us something interesting to look at," Wes gripes. "This is just...pathetic." He dismisses Gigi with a wave, but aside from her Dexid-induced swaying, she stands more or less still in front of a top-of-the-line six-burner stove, watching a pot of water boil. It's so dull, I almost feel bad for her.

Almost.

"Give her a chance," I say. "There's still time for a boiling bunny to make an appearance."

Wes snorts and nods a concession. "Her dream doesn't really matter anyway. We're not here to observe."

A knot tightens in my stomach.

"Yeah, but it'd be so much easier to do this if she was euthanizing puppies."

He straightens and wags a finger at me. "Don't you wimp out on me, Reyes," he says in an only slightly more playful than aggressive manner. He slides over to Gigi and stands close behind her, careful not to touch. "We agreed to take our super powers out for a test drive in a beat-up old jalopy so it wouldn't matter if we crashed it." His eyes give Gigi a once-over. "Here's the car. You've got the keys. What's the holdup?"

I let out a sigh.

"Eeh—" he says, like the buzzer at the end of a countdown clock. "Time's up."

And before I can blink, he jumps into Gigi's body.

The second he makes contact with her skin, he is part of her, pressing into her, the front of his body becoming one with the back of hers. Gigi stands at the stove, eyes glazed, mouth slack, arms outstretched, wrists limp. And Wes is sewn on. He is the master pulling the puppet's strings.

They walk backward.

Stop.

Turn left.

The extra Dexid we took must be working, because he has way more control of Gigi than I did of Grady. And while I, like every other normal person, am not a particular fan of mimes, this performance is riveting. Standing over something that's invisible to me, Wes uses Gigi's hands to travel over a flat surface, rifling through something that I cannot *imagine but that clearly has a powerful effect on him. Gigi's features tighten. Her hands ball into fists. Agitated, Wes scans invisible walls, stopping at different spots to get a closer look at items that cause his jaw, or rather, Gigi's jaw, to clench. He paces the room and roughly runs her fingers through her hair. He's trying to make sense of something entirely unknown to me, and it's making me feel like I've shown up late for a test.*

A full-moon howl coming from just outside Gigi's dream house steals my attention. The Burners have found us. I look out the kitchen window to where two hulking silhouettes peer in at me, their heavy, putrid breath fogging the glass. I should be terrified, and for a moment, I am. But once the initial shock of the Burners' presence wears off, I'm more worried than anything else. What if they come before Wes is finished with Gigi? What if I don't get my turn?

I move on instinct, first jogging then running full-out until I slam into Gigi and Wes.

Then...

Whoosh.
Pop.

I blink my eyes until they adjust to the dark of Gigi's bedroom, a place I know so well. I sit up to find that I'm already on the floor, and Wes is gone. Did he seize out? Or did I push him out of Gigi's body when I jumped in? Opposite me is a queen-size, pretty-in-pink bed, replete with satin tufted headboard and five-hundred-thread-count

Egyptian cotton sheets. Beside it is the framed poster of M.C. Escher's *Relativity* that was a souvenir from a trip we took to the Metropolitan Museum of Art just last fall. I stare at the picture, a reminder of happier times, and my shoulders slump.

It was her favorite piece, she'd said, because in it, the laws of physics didn't apply. There were no rules and no limits, two things Gigi was always trying to break. I'd told her that that was exactly why it freaked me out. So on our way out of the museum, she took me to the gift shop and bought us each a print. When she handed me mine, she said, "For when you get lost. Now we both have a map."

I laugh in Gigi's voice as I remember the conversation. Then my head begins to ache. What am I doing here? How can things have gotten to this awful place? Yes, Gigi's got a serious mean streak, but she's also the girl who once sat for hours with a freshman whose error cost us the game. Instead of blaming the girl, she told her stories about her own losses, building her back up so she could take the field with us the next day. Gigi's not a bad person. She's my friend.

Of course, friends don't play incriminating voice mails over the loud speaker at school or share pictures of you that she took without your consent. How can one mistake erase everything good we had? How can what I did really warrant all the venom Gigi is throwing my way?

It can't.

I get to my feet and look around. First thing I see is the bulletin board that hangs just outside her closet. As always, photos of Gigi and friends cover every inch of it. The last time I saw it, I'd been featured prominently. When I look now, I see that, though the same pictures I've always known are still there, I've been defaced in every one of them. Devil horns, Hitler moustaches, a blob of ink blacking me completely out. I haven't been erased from Gigi's life. I've become the evil demon that's infiltrated it and is going to be exorcised as painfully and publically as possible.

Fuming, I remember that whatever first upset Wes was on Gigi's desk, so I make a beeline for it. Immediately, I discover the source of his displeasure. Scattered across the desk are the pictures of me from the clinic. The ones she taped to my locker and so many more. Beside them are scissors and a glue stick. And covering all of it are little wisps of dark human hair.

My hair. The hair she took from me without permission. The hair she glued to a doll to shame me at school. To tell me I am not the sum of my parts but only this, a monster, a freak. That nothing else about me matters but my disorder, and that I do not count.

The tingling sensation that I felt inside Grady is tenfold now. Whether that's because of the extra Dexid, or because of the rage that's infected my every cell, or both, doesn't matter. I am in control. No rules. No limits.

I throw open her desk drawer and easily locate the

instrument of my revenge. I surrender to the moment and let fury guide me. Gripping the scissors in my right hand, I march over to Gigi's full-length mirror and regard her furious face as it stares back at me. Clutching a large section of her hair at the front, I draw the scissors to her roots and cut. Chunk after chunk, I lop off Gigi's long, flowing tresses until all that's left are uneven patches of mousy straw fuzz against a bright white scalp.

A pink lipstick stands at attention on her desk, just within reach. I grab it and, in big block letters, scrawl a message across the smooth glass.

Here's your karma, bitch.

Then I scream, take the self-standing mirror in both hands, throw my head back, and slam it into the frame.

Whoosh.

Pop.

*Back in Gigi's banal dream, Wes helps me to my feet. "Burners,"
he says, and I hear pounding against the patio door. I take one last
look at Gigi sitting on the floor, her long, beautiful hair now the thing
of dreams.*

I smile.

*Wes leads me out of the kitchen, and we escape through the garage.
The monsters are fierce, but they aren't particularly smart. As they search
the house for us, we take advantage of our head start. We run through
the dark fields that surround the home and just keep going.*

Hand in hand.
Never slowing.
Never tiring.
All through the night.

. . . .

"Three times. Three times, if you can believe it!" Tessa huffs as she flips through one of the glossy tabloids she subscribes to. "I mean that's some serious nerve to still be calling him her boyfriend after she's been caught making out with another guy, not once, but three times!"

"Mmm-hmm," I vaguely agree. Though I've long considered it part of my best friend duty to feign interest in the messed-up private lives of the movie starlets and celebutants that Tessa holds so dear, today, I can barely fake it. As we sit on the Quad soaking up the sun of the first March morning warm enough to be considered spring, my eyes scan the crowd of my classmates in search of the only person whose private life holds any interest for me.

At the far end of the green, Jamie and Meat toss a football as a trio of pom girls cheers them on. Not far from them, Amber's new hookup, Pete, is arguing with his recent ex Jenny, who looks like she hasn't eaten in days. By the garbage shed, our resident genius Amy Lawrence sits peacefully reading a book until Kiara (who may be a badass but is also a brain and Amy's lab partner) plops down beside her. Amy scrambles for something in her bag (a pen? her firstborn child?) as Kiara claps her on the shoulder too hard, looking like a clichéd after-school-special bully.

In other words, a day like any other for all of them. But not for me. And not for Wes. A torturous ache takes up residence in my chest, and it swells with every new arrival to the Quad. My knees jiggle. I'm picking my cuticles raw. Where is he?

"Sar," Tessa says, tossing her magazine at me. "This is not trivial stuff. I'm doing important sociological research into the lifestyles of the randomly rich and pointlessly famous! This is my future I'm cramming for here."

"Sorry," I say.

"It's cool." She shrugs. "You're usually pretty good at pretending you give a crap."

"I do," I lie. "My mind's just somewhere else."

Tessa reaches over her outstretched legs and retrieves the magazine she threw at me. "Somewhere else like the West Gate?" she teases.

The West Gate. How can I have been so stupid? Why did I think I'd find Wes here, in the Quad, when all our previous encounters have been over there? I shove my books into my bag and jump to my feet, the ache in my chest thumping in gleeful agony. "I have to go. I totally forgot where I'm supposed to be," I stammer.

"Supposed to be? Sarah, I was kidding. Homeroom's in five. You don't have time to go."

"I'll see you in class," I say, fumbling with the zipper of my bag. I'm in such a frantic rush that I begin walking before I've stood up. I make it one bent, twisted step before I plow right into a solid mass of flesh. I straighten up and am eye level with a flannel-clad, broad chest.

Large hands cup my face and lift my chin skyward. My eyes sweep up, past the taut jaw, above the full lips, beyond the crooked nose. They stop on the deep set, searching green eyes that sparkle wildly. The hands cradling my face tighten slightly and pull me forward.

Wes presses his lips onto mine, our mouths open, and I close my eyes.

My thighs go rigid, and I flex my feet. I wrap my arms around his back and pull him closer. He inhales deeply through his nose, gasping for air without taking his mouth from mine. Then he releases his grip on my face. One hand forages through my hair and, finding the back of my head, pushes me deeper into him as his other arm coils around my waist. I feast on him as he devours me. My back arches, and a small moan escapes from my lips. It's only a hint of indecency, but it's indecent nonetheless. I hope it's quiet enough so that only Wes hears. It's for no one but him.

If I had even the tiniest bit of my wits about me, the remote ability to consider anyone but myself in this moment, I might notice Tessa's gaping grin as she tries not to giggle at the sight of us. I might worry that Jamie will fumble the football as he sees me, and his heart will hurt. Might give a thought to the spectacle Wes and I are making and consider a modicum of decency. But I don't. There's nothing but Wes and me, and this most fan-freaking-tastic first kiss anyone could ever imagine.

Finally, days, weeks, years later, we pull apart. We look only at each other, no embarrassed side glances, just eyes, mouths, eyes again. His breath is ragged, and he licks his lips. I hear myself panting and don't even care as I flush. Wes holds out his hand, and I take it. His grip is firm and familiar, and he leads me into the building, eyes still trained on mine. It's amazing neither one of us walks into a wall or a trash can. But we're floating, gliding, drifting together as one. It's now just a fact.

Wes Nolan and I are destiny itself.

chapter fourteen

. . . .

If you could enter anyone's dream and sleepwalk in their body, who would it be?" Wes asks as he squints up at me, his head resting in my lap. We're lounging on the empty football field, near the goal line. We've cut all our classes for the day, and I couldn't care less. Between the warm wind, the spring-awakening grass, and my super dreamy new boyfriend, there's nowhere else I want to be. I shift slightly to block the sun from his eyes.

"Living or dead?" I ask.

"Either," he replies.

I consider this. "George Washington."

"George Washington? Seriously?"

"Why not?" I ask as he frowns.

"I mean, okay, he was the first president and all, but of

everyone in history to choose from, why a soldier who couldn't tell a lie and had bad teeth?"

I smile. "To see if he really slept everywhere they say he did."

Wes groans but can't hide his grin for long.

I lean down and kiss it. "What about you?"

"Easy," he says. "Freud. I mean, if he had that many crazy theories about people's thoughts and desires based on their dreams, his must've been freaking awesome."

"You're freaking awesome," I sing-song. As soon as the words escape into the ether, I cover my face. "I can't believe I just said that."

Wes sits up and pulls my hands down. "You're freaking awesome too," he says, smiling broadly. He tackles me. I scream, and he tickles until I cry uncle. As my giggle-gasps subside, I look up into his face hovering above mine. It's no longer playful or warm but dead serious. Hungry. I lick my lips and swallow hard. I start losing track of the public area we're in.

Then he kisses me. He kisses me and kisses me until it's so obvious where things are headed that we have no choice but to stop. He collapses beside me on the field, and I rest my head in the space between his chest and shoulder, staring up at the blue sky and the foamy clouds as they float by.

"We can do it, you know," he says wistfully. "I mean, not with dead people, obviously. But anyone alive that we have access to and can dose with Dexid—they're ours. And the more pills we take, the better we can control them. Last night proved it." He twirls my hair with his fingers. "Did you notice that when one of us was inside Gigi, the Burners stayed away? I don't think they can come near us when we're in a dreamer. God, this is great!"

I feel him tighten in the same way he did when we kissed. "We can follow the dreamer's mind and lead their bodies. Be anyone. Go anywhere. Do anything. Sarah, we are so…"

"Screwed," I say at the same time as he says, "Powerful."

"What? Screwed?" Wes untangles his legs from mine and sits up. Reluctantly, I do the same. "You're joking, right?" He laughs the way sane people do when confronted with the rantings of a crazy person. I look away from him and contemplate a newly sprouted blade of grass.

"We're warped," I say. "What we did last night—if we really did do it—was pretty messed up."

"If we really did do it?" he scoffs, completely ignoring my introduction of morality into the conversation. "What do you mean *if*? You saw Grady yesterday, and you were *inside* Gigi last night. I hate to break it to you, kid, but we've got superpowers. No amount of denial is going to change that, so why not fight the good fight?"

"The good fight?" I laugh. "Which part of the night was that? When we invaded a defenseless girl's privacy, or when I nearly scalped her?"

"Have you forgotten yesterday?" he says sharply. "The photos, the shrine? The hair missing from *your* head?" He reaches out and runs his hand over the significantly shorter section of hair just above my neck. I pull back.

Truth be told, I haven't let myself think too much about Gigi and what she did to me the day before or how I upped the ante last night. Ever since I woke up this morning, all I wanted to do was find Wes in real waking life and kiss him. A lot. Of course, I knew it was only a matter of time before the topic of Gigi and what we did came up. What I didn't anticipate was the utter glee with which Wes would recollect it.

"No, I haven't forgotten anything," I say. "But do you really think what happened last night was…"

I trail off, uncertain how to finish the thought. Am I unconvinced that it was real or that it was deserved? My blue-sky afternoon with Wes starts to feel overcast, and I fear he's going to run for cover. But to my surprise, he puffs out a long breath and pulls me to him.

"Okay, Sarah, okay," he whispers into my hair. "Let's not fight about this. We all process things in our own time. I'll give you yours." He kisses the top of my head and springs to his feet. Though he grins down at me, there's no hint of the smile in his eyes. "Listen, I've got a scheduling issue I'm supposed to fix with the program office before the end of the day. See you later?"

"Sure," I say with as much indifference as I can fake. "I've got a team meeting I should go to anyway."

Wes grabs his things and leans down to give me a kiss. It's soft and sweet but lacks the barely restrained lust that's characterized our previous ones. As he throws his messenger bag over his shoulder, he winks at me, then walks away. And just like that, the boy who couldn't keep his hands off me can't seem to put enough space between us. He's halfway across the football field before I can even wonder whether or not I want to run after him.

I sit on the grass for a while, not liking the loneliness his absence creates. After a few minutes, I gather my things and head toward the athletic center. Though I had every intention of skipping this meeting when an afternoon with Wes's eyes and lips and hands was the alternative, now that our clandestine encounter's been redacted, a little distraction seems like a good enough idea. It's likely Gigi will be there. She is our captain after all. But whether I'm ready to admit this to Wes or not, the triumph of last night has bolstered me a bit. Getting a little power back feels good.

As I swing open the doors of the girls' locker room, Kiara and Amber are waiting for me. A piece of paper reading *LAX MEETING CANCELED* is tacked to the bulletin board. The sick feeling of consequence punches me in the gut. I start to back away, but Kiara's hand shoots out and holds me tight.

Saying nothing, Gigi's groupies lead me along the rows of lockers. Though there's no mean-girl giggling, neither do they look triumphant. A mixture of anxiety and confusion marks both their expressions. And that makes me more nervous than anything else.

It's equally unnerving to see the locker room empty. Missing is the tangy, oppressive smell of steamy sweat; the community of girls lined in front of locker doors in various unselfconscious states of undress; the cacophony of smack talking and laughter echoing off the tiled walls. Unlike Hollywood's version of the locker room as sacrificial altar, mine has always been a safe haven in which I either prepare for battle or boast about my scars. Now it seems like the vacant ruins of a world from which I've been removed. I wonder if Hollywood has it right.

I move cautiously, half expecting Gigi (clad in a ski mask and toting a butcher's knife) to jump out at any time. But aside from the constant trickle of a leaky faucet, the gelatinous squishing noise that our sneakers make against the damp floor is the only sound. When I reach the end of the row, I turn toward the open area between the lockers and shower stalls.

I freeze.

Before me is a frail girl in sunglasses and a hoodie pulled up to cover her head. She stands slightly hunched with her arms crossed tight at her chest. At first, she doesn't look at me. I'm not even sure she knows I'm here as she whispers something to herself, rapidly and with barely a pause for breath. Her head shakes from side to side, a slow pendulum at first. But the movement grows until she's thrashing it about, like a child as he tries to shake off a bad dream.

Then she stops. Without looking directly at me, she takes off her sunglasses and pulls down her hood to reveal a black eye, uneven close-cropped hair, and a bald spot on the side of her head.

Amber gasps.

"Oh my God," says Kiara.

"Did you think this was a fashion statement?" Gigi snaps at

her friends, who have clearly and typically followed their leader's orders without questioning the why or what for. They've simply delivered me because Gigi asked. In this moment, I find these two way more sickening than their mean-girl master. But that may be due, at least in part, to how pathetic Gigi looks. I want to say something, to return to the Sarah from two days ago, the one with remorse. But I don't. I can't. I'm frightened and, to be honest, completely fascinated by the sight of what I've done. My dream came true. *I* made it happen. Gigi's the proof.

"It's real," I whisper in awe to myself.

Gigi sprints toward me, stopping just short of making actual physical contact. Kiara drops my arm as she and Amber take a step back.

"What did you say?" Gigi demands, her voice shrill, her words fast and jumbled together. I say nothing, only stare. Her eyes are beady as they dart around, searching my face, my body, for something. An answer? A clue? Gigi's crossed arms tighten, and her hands pulse as they grip her biceps. She looks utterly unhinged. Then she closes her eyes and takes a cleansing breath. It's a ritual I've seen her do a thousand times when faced with a particularly tough opponent just before she eats her for lunch.

When she opens her eyes again, she's the tough, uncompromising, game-day thug I know. Staring me down, the fury of a bull spitting out from her flared nostrils, Gigi thrusts her face up in mine.

"How did you do it?" she demands through locked jaws.

"Did you drug me? Sneak into my room? Tell me, Sarah, because it was you. I saw the note. I know. I know it was you."

I open my mouth to speak, but what on earth can I say? She's right. It was me. I did this to her. When I don't say anything, she goes on.

"You know, I never should have bothered with you. From the first day of peewees, my mother told me to steer clear." She nods manically. "Oh yeah, she'd heard about you. Every parent had. Creepy little Sarah Reyes who didn't have a daddy and couldn't have sleepovers. They knew something was up but obviously not the full extent, otherwise this," she says, wagging her pointer finger between us, "you and me, never would have happened. But you were good with a stick, so I gave you a chance." She begins to run her fingers through her hair but stops when she remembers it's almost all gone. In a flash, Gigi's lecture loses its language as rage tightens her features, and her hands shoot forward. She shoves me backward, knocking the wind out of me before I have the slightest chance to defend myself.

"Gigi, wait," Amber says as Kiara puts her hand on her captain's shoulder. Gigi knocks it off, and her lieutenants stand down. She pins me to a locker. Her face is inches from mine.

"I made your crappy life tolerable," she yells. "I pretended you weren't a total weirdo. What a mistake that was. I bet Jamie's accident last year wasn't even an accident at all. I wouldn't be surprised if it was you who actually broke his nose."

I flinch. Without intending to, Gigi's delivered a serious blow below the belt. And she sees it. Her ranting instantly quells, and her face lights up like she's just been accepted to Amherst. "Oh my God. You totally did it. He covered for you. You didn't just do this to me—you did it to Jamie too!" She cackles like a mean-girl Wicked Witch of the West as she loosens her grip. "Did you blame it on your sleep? Was that your bullshit defense then too?"

I turn my head, but Gigi grabs my chin and yanks my face to meet hers. In the background, Kiara and Amber look at each other, uncomfortable and unsure. "How do you do it?" she demands. "How do you get away with everything? Why do I get detention for showing everyone the freak show you really are and you get...people watching you sleep? Tell me, Sarah, tell me, or I will make you pay in ways you can't even imagine."

"How?" I hiss. "By defacing me in all your pictures of us?"

Her face lifts in triumph. "I knew it!" she cries. "You *were* in my room last night. How else would you have seen the pictures?"

I drop my eyes. Crap.

Gigi smiles, savoring this bit of power at last. "You think you're so special. Well, I've got news for you. They call every reject 'special' now. It's just a pretty way of saying you do not belong, you are not normal. And I'm going to make sure that everyone finally knows it.

"Amber," she barks. "Record this."

Gigi's frightened lap dog fumbles with her phone and begins videoing my confession.

"Tell me how, Sarah," Gigi says in the contrived whimpering tone of a wounded innocent. "How did you get into my room last night? How did you keep me still while you violated me? I was supposed to be safe in my bed, safe while I slept."

She was supposed to be safe in *her* bed? Safe while *she* slept? I don't know if it's imagining the audience that'll be suckered into believing this shift in her persona or the sheer hypocrisy of her accusations after what she and Josh did to me at the clinic just two nights before, but I'm done. Wes is right. Gigi is no innocent. Any guilt I have about what happened last night vanishes. I might not be a victim, but neither is she. I lean forward and speak so only she can hear. "Not your room. I didn't break into your room. But that was a nice kitchen. Did the water ever boil?"

Gigi drops her hand like I'm on fire and stumbles backward. Kiara moves toward me but doesn't come between us, confused by Gigi's sudden retreat.

I take a step forward. "You didn't think you were alone in that big empty house, did you?" I whisper. "There was something else there too. Wasn't there? Something in the shadows. It's waiting for you. Watching you. Coming for you."

Gigi's eyes are unblinking and wide. For a moment, I feel strength in this small victory. I'm a fool not to realize it will be short-lived.

With no preamble, my tormented tormentor screams and charges at me full force. Grabbing my hair by the roots, she slams my head back against the locker door. I try to lift my arms, to protect my aching skull by helmeting my head with my limbs, but Gigi is relentless. Once again, I'm trapped, unable to defend my body as my brain scrambles, valiantly but fruitlessly, to help.

All I can do is watch through blurred vision as she wraps her middle and pointer fingers around the bottom loop of my hoop earring and tears it out.

I cry out, and Gigi lets me fall to the ground. I steady my upper body on my right arm as my free hand clutches at my bleeding lobe. The sticky warmth of blood trickles through my fingers, and I watch it drip onto the tile beneath me.

Kiara and Amber just stand there, gaping. Though they haven't added to the blows, Amber's phone is still recording, and neither has tried to help.

Gigi towers over me, shaking, breathing hard, spent. My stomach clenches. Then she kneels beside my bloody ear and, her voice trembling, whispers, "Stay away from me, you freak." She turns and leaves me crying as Kiara and Amber follow her out.

chapter fifteen

. . . .

W es doesn't say much after his initial horrified reaction to my bandaged ear. And I'm too shell-shocked to speak. So we walk in relative silence back to my house.

Our first time alone together in my room isn't exactly how I pictured it. Wes perches on my windowsill, staring out at the sunny day that now seems to be mocking us. I lean against the doorframe at the entrance. Even though it's my space, something about Wes's demeanor, contemplating so deeply, utterly lost in his own thoughts, makes me feel as though I should wait for an invitation.

"High school sucks," he says finally, still staring out the window. "And I should know. I've been to enough different ones to be considered an expert."

I relax a bit and move to the edge of my bed.

"Do you remember who you were last week?" he asks.

"Uh, Sarah Reyes?" I venture.

"No. You were Gigi."

My body jerks back as if I've been slapped. I begin to protest, but he holds up a hand to silence me. "The first time I saw you wasn't in a dream. It was a week before at school, when I was doing my paperwork for enrollment. You were strutting down the halls like you owned them. Smiling at everyone you passed, then laughing at whatever remark Gigi made as soon as they were out of earshot." He shakes his head. "I'm sorry to say it, but in some ways, you were even worse. Because you know what it's like to be imperfect. Imperfect in a way that trumps any unibrow or lisp."

"Well, if I'm so terrible," I say, "why are you hanging out with me?" Though my words are accusatory, it strikes me that I could just as easily be challenging myself as him. It's not like I don't get exactly what he's talking about. In the past few days, I've experienced what it's like to be on the receiving end of Gigi's ire, and my own culpability in her past cruelties toward others has been creeping on me bad. I've been so afraid of slipping from my rung on the high school social ladder that I've allowed for too much bad behavior, and it makes me sick. But hearing Wes say it is way worse. Guilt and rage collide inside of me, and I clutch my stomach.

"I'm hanging out with you," Wes says, "because you're not that girl anymore. You've fallen from your pedestal, but you're still standing. You're not knocking innocent people down to build yourself back up, but you're not being a total pushover either. You, Sarah Reyes, are a force of nature." A half grin lightens his face. "And if you start using those powers for good— that's the kind of girl I can get behind."

"Thanks, I guess." Though my mumbled retort gives nothing away, inside, I'm relieved to be forgiven by someone, and I thrill at this vision of the new me.

"Tell me something," he says as he leans forward. "How'd it feel seeing Gigi knocked down a peg today?"

"It didn't feel great." I pout, pointing at my ear.

"Fair enough," he says. "But what she did to you is how you know she's scared. Tell me you don't believe that she'll think twice before messing with someone else."

I allow a slight smile. Wes's own grin grows.

"I think you did good today," he says and tips an invisible hat. I continue to thaw. "I'd even say you made up for a few of those ignored victims of Gigi MacDonald's too." He places his hands behind his head and leans against the window frame. Surveying my room, he nods. "But what if we could do better?"

"Meaning?"

"Way I see it, we've got two great tastes that taste great together: our awesome new abilities that we've just scratched the surface of and a duty to do something about the hell that is our high school existence. So why not use the one to work out the other?"

"I still don't follow," I say.

Wes clasps his hands together. "It's a widely accepted fact

that high school is the worst, right? Either you're just finding a way to survive it before moving onto college and a better life, or it's the pinnacle of your existence, and once you graduate, nothing lives up to your big win at regionals or your Jennifer Aniston hair at prom.

"But what if it didn't have to be like that? What if there was something between kissing the class ring and getting drenched in pig's blood? What if you could walk into school like you owned the place without having to make everyone else feel like they couldn't make rent? *We* could do that, Sarah. *We* could bring down the monarchy and let the people eat cake."

"How?" I laugh. "By terrorizing them in their sleep?"

"Yes," he says, and the utter lack of humor in his voice shuts me right up.

"No. Come on," I manage finally. "Even if what I did to Gigi last night scared her, she was also way more antagonistic than I've seen her to date."

"If it starts to become clear that bad behavior has consequence, things will change," he says. "Don't those two stooges of hers deserve a little payback? From what I hear, you're not the only one they've messed with."

I can't deny that Wes has a point. While there's absolutely no arguing that Kiara's a rotten egg, Amber actually feels like the worst of the two. And it's not just because, unlike Kiara, Amber and I were actually friends. While I know I've been guilty of turning a blind eye to many of Gigi's bad deeds, Amber has consistently participated. She's like a demented Marcy to Gigi's

Peppermint Patty, all "yes, sirs" with no questions asked. Is she that terrified of a life outside of Gigi's inner circle? Of returning to those lonely middle school weekends? Probably. But I'm sick of fear justifying cruelty. Just because dating Pete temporarily pacifies the ghost of thirteen-year-old Acne Amber doesn't mean she isn't responsible for the damage she leaves in her wake. I imagine Amber being forced to deal with the repercussions of her actions, and I smile.

Wes kneels before me. "We've got some serious stuff going on with what we can do in dreams, and we need to keep learning how to control it. So why not here? Why not be all that we can be while making our high school a better place?"

I stop smiling and pull away slightly. "You realize that you're talking about experimenting on our classmates?"

"Only the shitty ones," he clarifies.

"Oh, well then," I say with a snort. "Seriously, this coming from you, Patient Zero?"

He frowns. "That's not fair, Sarah. One well-deserved karmic nightmare is not the same as being child labor for Big Pharma."

I flush as he goes on.

"But if you want to go there, okay. The history of scientific breakthrough is full of questionable labs. Would you deny the results just because you're queasy about the means?"

"Uh, ya, Herr Doctor." I salute.

"Nice. Go for the Nazi reference," he says, rolling his eyes. "How about something less obvious. You know, we have the vaccine for tuberculosis because two prison inmates in Colorado were the first human test subjects. They got released for their trouble. Seems like a fair trade to me. And what about the cute and fuzzy animals getting injected with cancer while we keep poisoning our bodies, because soon enough, thanks to Fluffy the rabbit, we'll be able to cure all the self-inflicted damage? I don't hear anyone refusing chemo because of that.

"Not to mention if it weren't for all the testing that's been done on me, we wouldn't finally have the one drug that keeps our bodies still at night. I might not be thrilled to have been the rat, but that's all the more reason I should get to enjoy where I am now." He rests his hands on my knees. "And I'm not complaining about having found you because of it either."

I look away, not ready to give in yet but already feeling myself pulled in his direction.

"I'm not talking about doing any real damage," he says in a low voice, soft and smooth. "I'm just suggesting that we take advantage of some teachable moments with the tools at our disposal. On balance, I'd say there's less harm in that than there is in leaving Gigi and the like to continue their reign of destruction unchecked. Especially now that we know we can do something about it." He places his fingers on my chin and turns my face to meet his. "You know what they say about great power, right? Don't you think it's our responsibility?"

He inserts his body between my legs so that my thighs hug his rib cage. "You've been denying a part of yourself in order to avoid being laughed at, or worse. And now that the 'or worse' has happened, are you going to run away and hide? Sarah," he says hotly, his face inching closer to mine. "Tell me you won't go back to being that half person. Tell me you're ready to be exactly who you are, all of you. Tell me you're strong enough to do this. Make it up to everyone you ever let feel the way you've felt this past week. Be the girl I know you really are."

His hands creep up my legs, around my waist, and land on my back. Our positions equalize our heights, and his mouth moves forward until it's nearly touching mine.

Then he waits.

A hungry little grin curls the corners of my mouth. For the first time since I can remember, I'm not being seen as some disorder that needs to be fixed but as someone special with infinite potential. What if the brave new version of me that Wes sees so clearly is the girl who's been here all along? I've been tracing her in every acceptable avenue available to me—school, dating, sports—but I've been too scared to follow the unbeaten path that every molecule in my body has been begging to forge. Until now.

A moan of affirmation escapes my lips as they press against Wes's, and then I'm dragging him down the rabbit hole with me, no longer lost, but exploring, in search of our very own Wonderland. Every kiss, every touch serves as our covenant this afternoon. I will no longer be the girl who's ashamed. I'll embrace my power and use it to do better, to be better.

Of course, better is a subjective term. Just like one person's dream is another one's nightmare.

chapter sixteen

· ·

The rest of the week is a flurry of possession and punishment. While I'm tasked with getting my hands on Grady's supply, Wes takes care of dosing our marks. When I ask my new boyfriend-slash-accomplice how he intends to slip our victims the Dexid, he darkly jokes that the only thing he learned from those tony boarding school jerks was how to slip a girl a roofie undetected. Then he tells me not to worry about it and distracts me with inappropriate touching, which is fine by me. Truth is, though I should care how he does it, I don't. For the first time in ages, I'm all in with a full house, and I want to win.

The little tease of spring weather has been replaced by yet another cold front and gray skies. I jog in place to keep warm as I wait for Grady outside his sixth period gym class. Ever since I've known him, the genius with zero athletic ability has found a way to avoid any sort of P. E. participation. Rumor is he's got a deal with a kid in the attendance office that, in exchange for some hard-to-trace substances, Grady only needs to be present for roll call at the start of class and then he can go on his merry way. It sounds like an urban legend, but the more deeply I entrench myself in shady doings and unbelievable truths, the easier it is to believe anything about anybody.

Three minutes after the bell rings, Grady exits the athletic center and walks in my direction. "Where's Heathcliff?" he asks as he approaches. "Trolling the moors?"

"Wes is not that moody," I say with a chuckle. "We were having an off day when you saw us. Sorry I was a little intense about the Dexid and Josh."

Grady shrugs. "Eh, you're usually pretty okay."

"Thanks," I say. "But I think you might be in the minority with that opinion."

Grady raises his eyebrows. "I don't judge friends, Sarah," he says.

And I feel like a royal schmuck. While I don't know Grady super well, he was around a lot when I was dating Jamie, as we often hung out at Meat's house. Unlike every other male jock at IHS—including Meat—Jamie has always been nice to Grady. So by association, I guess I'm okay in his book too. And while I've certainly never been mean to him, neither have I done enough by half to deserve his kindness. I kiss him on the cheek and smile as his skin flushes orange to match his hair.

He pulls a small vial with about a dozen little gold pills in it from his pocket. But as I reach for it, he snatches it back. "Before I hand this over, are you really sure you want it? I've told you I don't know the full range of side effects. And what I've personally experienced wasn't so nice."

"Trust me," I say. "I know what I'm doing."

He grimaces. "If I had a nickel for every time I heard someone say that…"

"You still wouldn't have as much money as you do from selling drugs," I say. I slap a wad of cash into his empty hand and take the bottle of pills from the other. "I appreciate the concern, Grady. I truly do. But I promise I'll be fine."

He stuffs the money into his pocket and adjusts his taped glasses. "Make your boyfriend take it first, okay? So you'll know not to if he drops dead."

I laugh. "That's friendly."

Grady shrugs. "I don't really care what happens to him. See you around, Sarah." Then he turns and walks away. For all my glossing over Grady's drug dealing, there's a darkness to it that I never really considered. Grady sells drugs because he honestly doesn't care about the people who take them. And why would he when they've done way worse to him over the years than not give a crap?

I curl my fingers around the bottle of Dexid. *Things are going to get better for kids like Grady*, I tell myself. I leave the athletic center feeling as though Wes and I truly are doing a public service.

I've scored ten pills off Grady. That night, we use five: two for Wes and two for me to add to the pill we get at the clinic. The last one is for Kiara.

I review our plan, treat it like a play from a playbook, repeat it until I know it by heart. The set up: drug Kiara, dose ourselves with extra pills to get even better control, find Kiara in Grand Central, follow her into her dream. Then for the main event: jump into her commuter body in the dream and wake up in her actual, flesh-and-blood body in real life. Control her, make her do what I want. And when I'm finished with her, exit her sleeping carcass and return to the train station.

Whether it's the anticipation of a perfectly planned attack or the addition of yet another pill, I can't say, but my body feels electric as I lie on the cot at the clinic, waiting for the Dexid to kick in.

Heat emanates from my skin.

Static crackles at my fingertips.

Electricity pulses beneath my eyelids as

they…

slide…

shut.

. . . .

I come to in the station. Wes is already waiting for me, a smile that's more dopey than dangerous plastered on his face. It matches mine. We come together behind a tottering Kiara and, hand in hand, we follow her into her dream.

It's a gothic rave where thumping music meets weeping angels and gargoyled cathedral spires. Though I know her as a party girl and bully, Kiara's super religious and overachieving tiger mom and professor dad have always seen their little straight-A student in the unblemished white that she wore at her first communion.

"I think this girl has some serious issues to work out," I say as Wes leads me through the sweaty crowds to a pulpit where Kiara is dancing seductively with a priest.

"Ready?" he asks.

I nod, and he pulls me to him for one final intoxicating kiss. Then he shoves me backward

and I free-fall

into Kiara's body.

<gasp>

That first gulp of air after you've become someone else is frantic. By the time you acknowledge that your whole being has just contracted into what seems like an infinitesimally tiny ball, it is already expanding again, birthing into the unfamiliar shape of someone other than you. In an instant, you must learn to see through their eyes, touch with their skin, and breathe with their lungs. I can only imagine that this breath is akin to that of a newborn baby, trying out this oxygen thing for the first time. It is desperate, painful, confusing, and, above all, terrifying, because what if it doesn't work?

But then it does.

My gasps turn to even breathing, and it's time to get down to business. I throw off Kiara's covers and go straight for the bottle of Jack that I remember she used to boast she kept in a shoebox at the back of her closet. The plan is to expose her for the heathen that she is. To get her so plastered that, when her parents find her in a less than saintly position, they send her away for conversion therapy or an exorcism. If I can find a diary that exposes some of her less-than-Christian acts, all the better. But as I rummage around for her stash, I come across something way more damning.

Hidden beneath a pile of Bible camp T-shirts is a legal-size metal box secured by a tiny diary lock. I grab a nail file from Kiara's dresser and jimmy the lock open in no time. It strikes me that a girl on track to being named salutatorian should be smarter than to use such a flimsy lock, but when I see what's inside, all other thoughts flee.

If there's one place Kiara Taylor's parents want their daughter to get into more than heaven, it's Harvard. I never questioned Kiara's good grades or Ivy League ambitions. Almost all the girls on my team are fierce competitors in sports and academics. But as I sit in her body on the floor of her closet and sort through paper after paper of stolen answer keys and essays written by other people, I realize what a long con she's been playing.

There's pre-calc homework forged by the mathletes, civics papers from the valedictorian. There's even a poetry assignment written by the sophomore who Kickstarted our new lit magazine. And a sheet of paper I can only describe as a ledger matching every IHS student Kiara's bullied into letting her cheat off them to the work they've done on her behalf. When did she graduate from taking kid's lunch money to shaking them down for their smarts?

Instinctively, I grab her phone and hold it above the trove of incriminating evidence. But as my finger hovers over the camera icon, I pause. Judging from her ledger, Kiara's been using our classmates for years. If I expose her, won't I be damning them too?

The clock on her phone advances another minute. I have to make a decision. So I do as Kiara would.

I snap pictures of every bit of evidence there is. Then I upload everything that doesn't specifically mention her accomplice-victims by name to her Facebook account under the post, "Let the punishment fit the crime." Everything else, including the ledger, I e-mail to Wes, being sure to delete the sent e-mail so she can't track his involvement. Then I write Kiara an e-mail from her own account to herself: Bring anyone else down with you, and we'll post the rest.

I hit send and toss her phone onto her bed. I gather up all the papers and stuff them back in the metal box, careful to return it to its hiding place at the back of her closet. As I return to the open space of her bedroom, I catch sight of us in a mirror. Defiantly, I look directly at the gorgon whose head I've just lopped off.

I sit back on Kiara's bed and wait to leave her body and return to her dream.

I wait.

And wait.

There's no twinge of a seizure, no hint of an exit. I start to panic. Is it the extra Dexid that's keeping me here, tethered to Kiara's reality when I just want to get out? I get up and pace the room. What if her parents come in? What if I get stuck inside Kiara and can never escape? Would I have to be her forever? I kick myself for ignoring Grady's warning, for my hubris in thinking I had everything figured out. I doubled down on a drug that I know absolutely nothing about. Scratch that. I know plenty about it, and none of it is good. How could I be so stupid as to take the drug that makes me conscious in unconsciousness, that allows me to body-snatch my classmates and ask for more, please? I have offended the gods, and my punishment is to be trapped in the body of a bully-hypocrite-cheater for the rest of my life.

My jaw locks, and my chest constricts. I try to calm myself with deep breaths, but my breathing is simply too erratic to get a lock on. Think, Sarah, think. Was there something that brought on the seizure when I was in Grady's body? Anything I saw when Wes sent Gigi into an epileptic fit? Fear? Distress? Check to both, but I am still here. What about Gigi? What was I feeling when I began to shake out of her—

I stop pacing. I didn't exit Gigi's body the same way I

left Grady's. In Gigi's dream-walk, I was mad. I fought my way out.

I turn and walk to the far end of Kiara's room, gearing up for the self-inflicted violent act that will separate me from my host. Then, in one utterly graceless move, I hurl her figure at the wall, tripping on my way and knocking myself out of her body as her head crashes into the blush-colored sheetrock.

Whoosh.

Pop.

I am back in Kiara's dream. Wes is hovering near me, keeping a solid distance between himself and the two Burners that are lurking on the dance floor. Grabbing his hand, we run from them, through the crowd and out of the church-cum-club into the street-lamped twilight of an eroding metropolis.

As it was in Gigi's dream, the more distance we put between us and the dreamer, the less the Burners seem inclined to follow. When we are far enough away, I pull Wes down a deserted alley and shove him against a damp concrete wall. The rush of revenge—and getting away with it—turns me into a predator. Wes has no complaints.

We kiss and pant and fumble and grunt until waking separates us.

chapter seventeen

At school, everyone's talking about Kiara's confession. I'm running late from the clinic, so I don't make it in time to see her escorted from first period English to the principal's office. But as it turns out, I've only missed the coming attractions.

Wes intercepts me on my way to homeroom and leads me toward the admin office, where we loiter at the far end of an unusually crowded hallway. While some of the kids legitimately have to be there because their lockers are located in what's suddenly become prime real estate, most of our fellow gawkers are like us: desperate for a ticket to the circus.

A miserable-looking Kiara sits on a bench just outside the office as Principal Hatch ushers her parents inside. Though she surveys the crowd with a fierce evil eye and, at one point, even puffs out her chest and snarls an intimidating, "What're you looking at," no one backs away.

While everyone is fixated on what's about to emerge from the office though, a tornado strikes from the opposite direction. Amy Lawrence, valedictorian and author of many of Kiara's forged essays, comes stomping down the hall.

Her cheeks are flushed, and her ponytail's coming loose. She stops beside Kiara, her legs shaking so violently, it's a wonder she can stand. The whole crowd inches forward.

"Why would you do this?" Amy hisses. "Why would you go public?"

"Are you stupid?" Kiara snaps. "Obviously, someone found my stuff and uploaded it. Was it you?"

"What?" Amy cries in disbelief. "If they find out about me, I'm in as much trouble as you are!"

"You're right," Kiara says flatly. "You are."

Though I can see Kiara's threat for the impotent, last ditch power play it is, to the already tightly wound, type-A Amy, it's the final straw that doesn't just break the camel's back but defiles, eviscerates, and desecrates it.

"You can't," she shrieks. "You can't do this to me. I could get suspended! I've done everything you've ever told me to. You can't take my future away from me. I won't let you. I won't—"

"Shut up," Kiara says, getting to her feet. She towers over the girl, who flinches, but it turns out there's no need. Kiara's shoulders are hunched, her hands clasped tightly at her chest, as if in prayer. Her lips are dry, her eyes pleading. For once, Kiara

Taylor isn't scary but scared. "No one's going to suspend you. I destroyed all the evidence, okay? I'm not going to say anything. No one is. There's no proof, so if we all deny it, it'll be like this never happened, and everything will go back to the way it was in time for midterms."

I stop breathing. Is it possible? Will Kiara walk free?

As if answering my silent query, Amy shakes her head. "Back to the way it was for midterms?" she asks. "No. I'm not going back." She turns to address the crowd. "The first time Kiara copied my homework was in fifth grade. After I told my parents, she broke my glasses on the school bus for being a snitch." She looks back at Kiara. "You told me to tell them I tripped or the next time you'd break my wrist. So I did, and after that, you owned me. I've done everything you've told me to every day since. For almost eight years. Eight years! Well, now it's over."

We all stare, stunned, trying to process what Amy's saying. Could she actually be threatening Kiara? Could it be that, by simply articulating the truth of the way things work around here, the meanest of mean girls has unwittingly pushed Amy over the edge of hysteria and into the valley of blind courage? As the valedictorian moves toward the door of the office, Kiara grabs her arm. I take a step toward them, but Wes holds me back.

"Please," Kiara pleads. "Please help me." Her voice is shaking. She begins to cry. "You don't know what it's like. You don't know my parents. The pressure I'm under. What they'll do if they find out. I'm begging you, Amy. Please."

Kiara isn't a good enough actress to be faking this. And even I feel a pang of empathy tug at my breast.

But Amy has endured too much abuse to be moved. She yanks her arm free and says, "Tough. You're right. I probably won't get suspended. But even if I do? It'll be worth it if it gets rid of you. Besides, I'm guessing that once I tell them about the years of psychological torture and physical intimidation I've suffered at your hands, I won't even get a slap on the wrist. Who knows?" she says with sudden, surprising sass. "Maybe if I throw in a nervous breakdown, I'll get an extra free period."

Amy straightens. "I can't believe I forgot that I'm the smart one. And you, Kiara," she says as she smooths her ponytail. "You're done."

With that, Amy throws open the office door and marches inside.

Kiara stares at the spot where Amy stood in disbelief. I wonder if I should feel bad that she's going to be implicated in Kiara's takedown. But as I watch the smartest girl I know stand taller than ever before, I am convinced she's going to be more than all right. Amy Lawrence has blossomed into a badass in front of my very eyes.

Kiara doesn't move. She stares at the office, catatonic.

And we can't have that.

I catcall from the far end of the hall, and she snaps her head in my direction. Raising my phone, I take a picture. I wave good-bye as Wes slips his arm around my waist, and we strut off to homeroom.

"One down, one to go," he growls into my ear once we're out of sight.

"This totally turns you on, doesn't it?" I tease.

"Mean girls getting schooled? I can take it or leave it. What turns me on," he says as we round a corner and he pulls me to a row of deserted lockers, "is seeing you on a power trip." He gently pushes me against a locker and brings his lips to my neck but doesn't touch. They hover less than an inch away from my skin, and my toes curl in that blissful agony of anticipation. "No qualms, no regrets, all Dark Phoenix." He exhales hotly, and my skin is on fire. "Guys who can't get behind a powerful woman have no idea what they're missing."

I close my eyes as his mouth lands on my skin and the tips of his teeth nip at my neck.

"Tonight," he whispers between nibbles. "Let's do four pills. Really get in there. Do some damage."

"I think we're doing plenty of damage," I purr. "Three was pretty intense."

"Pfft," his breath dismisses. "What's a little nightmare in exchange for making your real-life dreams come true? The low may be sub-basement, but the high is a mile above the Empire State Building. Let's see what we're really capable of." Suddenly, his nuzzling stops cold. He pulls his mouth away and looks at me, perplexed eyes through thick lashes. "Unless you're afraid you can't handle it?"

I know instantly that he's calling me chicken. That he's using the oldest trick in the book to get me to do what he wants. I know I am smarter than this, and so my first instinct is to dig in my heels and be the living embodiment of the reverse psychology fail. But the truth is, I am kind of curious about what more Dexid might feel like. The extra surge of control that just a couple more pills gave me turned out to be the difference between an awkward bump and grind in Grady's body and the graceful choreography of Gigi and Kiara's sleepwalking ballets. And now that I know how to get myself out of the dreamer's body, why not give it a try? Why not find out what I can do with more of this wonder drug in my system? So I say, "Four it is." And I pull Wes's mouth to mine and choke down any reservations.

It only takes a moment of making out until I am once again losing track of our environment. Then a throat clears beside me. Mrs. French stands in the doorway of my homeroom, looking about as interested in teenaged lust as I am with her insistence that taupe is a legitimate color.

Wes takes his time pulling away from me and says, "See you in my dreams."

When I finally, reluctantly, let his hand go, I stride into the classroom, past Mrs. French as if she isn't even there.

Parking myself at my regular seat for the remaining five minutes of homeroom, I pull out my cell phone and bring up the photo of Kiara, playing with different filters in an effort to best highlight her fall from grace. I'm laughing at a particularly comedic manga version of the scene when someone says, "Oh good. I need a laugh. What've you got?"

Jamie leans over me, planting his hands on the back of my chair, and I look up into his eagerly smiling face.

"I call it *Mean Girls: They're Just Like Us!*" I say, laughing.

He cringes.

"What?"

"Nothing," he replies. "It's just, I didn't think you'd get such a kick out of seeing someone publically flogged, given recent events."

"Uh, it's Kiara," I snarl. "I think I can make an exception in her case."

Jamie doesn't say anything.

"Look, if anyone has it coming, it's her," I continue. "Did you know she's been shaking down Amy Lawrence since middle school? Poor girl's a wreck. I just saw her go into Hatch's office to confess everything."

"Whoa," he says. "That's awful. Middle school? That's years. I can't believe how many people are going to be hurt by this."

"You mean by Kiara," I correct, my tone acidic. "Hurt by Kiara."

"Well, yeah," he says, shrugging. "Including Kiara. She's pretty much screwed up her own life too."

I do not bother to stifle my guffaw. "Spare me, Jamie," I say dismissively. "She's the villain. Seriously, why are you so concerned about her? I feel like every time I see you lately, you're defending everyone I hate and telling me I should feel sorry for them."

"And I feel like every time we talk, you're using words like *hate* and displaying a stunning lack of sympathy for people you used to call friends."

I spit an incredulous puff of air but can find no words to accompany it. Jamie and I have had disagreements before, but I've never felt judged by him. He shakes his head at me and says, "I'm sorry for all the crap you've had to eat lately, but I'd have thought you'd develop empathy from it, not rage."

Just then, the bell rings, and he walks away from me.

I feel a slight tug to run after him and hash this out, but it's nothing compared to the righteous anger I feel at being so misunderstood. How did this become about me and my shortcomings? Kiara's the monster here. I shake my head and embrace a disappointment in Jamie that I'm entirely unused to. It's easy to sing "Kumbaya" when your life has only ever known harmony, but when yours is a song of dissonance, what's wrong with occasionally indulging in a good old minor second?

I grab my stuff and head off to my next class. Ahead of me, I spot Amber walking alone into chem lab. Wes's words echo in my mind.

One down, one to go.

I follow her into the classroom. She notices me staring and throws me her best scowl, but I don't look away. Silently, I wish her sweet dreams tonight. And I smile, knowing that it won't make a difference once I'm done with her.

chapter eighteen

While Kiara's demise was handed to us on a silver platter, Amber's proving to be a harder target. Gigi's vanity and Kiara's secret life were clear Achilles' heels to exploit, but with Amber, what you see is pretty much what you get. The best we can hope for is to totally freak her out with a proper haunting and irrefutable proof of it.

The previous night was my last in the clinic. This morning, I was released from observation with a slap on the back and a prescription. So tonight's my first chance to see how the Dexid works from the comfort of my own bed.

After a "Yay, You Sleep Like the Dead" celebratory dinner with my mom, I climb the stairs to my room. The nylon restraints that decorate the four quadrants of my bed lie open, awaiting my arrival to justify their existence. For a moment, I consider using them as backup, just in case. But as quickly as the thought ripens in my mind, it rots. The concept of *just in case* feels like a betrayal—to Wes, to the new me. There are no safety nets for what we're doing and no going back. Like the strong, fearless young woman I am, I stick out my tongue at the restraints and pop four Dexid: two from Grady's stash and two from my very own prescription bottle. For the first time since I was a kid, I get into my own bed and prepare for a peaceful night's sleep.

Peaceful is not what comes next.

My body thickens, expands, weighs down heavily on the softness of my bed. I feel my cheeks and throat marshmallow-puff out until my eyelids shut closed and there's no room for my breath. My arms, my legs, my torso are all swallowed whole, sucked into the quicksand of the duvet. I am absorbed into the suffocating foam of the mattress.

There is nothing left.

Then…

<gasp>

I awake in the station, relieved to have survived being eaten alive by my bed. Is this what sleeping at home will be like from now on? Or is it the four Dexid playing cruel tricks on me? I find Wes, who is as excited as ever, and I decide not to mention my man-eating mattress for now. We get to work.

We locate Amber, pursue her onto the train, stalk her into her dream, and…

Invade

her

body.

The clock reads 1:15 a.m. on Amber's computer, which I've just brought to blinding LED life with the click of a mouse. Her webpage is already open, and her ever-present webcam begins live streaming me, as Amber, sleepy eyed but ready for my close-up.

Or am I?

My eyes aren't adjusting to the computer light like they should. I squint at it in an effort to dull the searing black spots that come from looking at it for too long. The tingling sensation that accompanied my previous spirit walks now burns my flesh, converting the once-pleasurable electric hum into a crackling alarm. This body itches, feels too tight.

Everything is off tonight, from being devoured by my duvet to feeling like a donor organ that's been rejected by its new host. I want out. Now.

I notice a heavy paperweight beside the computer and for a second actually consider using it to knock myself out of this place, when a pubescent male voice chirps behind me.

"What are you doing?" Amber's pimply faced, beanpole of a stepbrother, Matt, asks as he enters the room. Matt is the one remnant of Amber's past that she can't escape. They were loser lovebirds for a week in fifth grade until their parents started dating. Suddenly, what was likely the only good thing in either of their social lives became fodder for some seriously gross teasing. Matt was all I could think of that might make Amber squirm.

I step away from the desk, tucking my fisted hands

behind my back, and stare at him. My scalp is throbbing. I want to rip all the itchy hair out. I don't know how much longer I can maintain this self-control.

Then I see that half-cocked grin of Wes's as it spreads across Matt's brace-face. I relax.

Though the plan had been for Wes to overtake Matt's sleeping body all along, it's a relief to see a sign of him inside there. I leap to my feet, ready to throw myself/Amber at him, but he raises a hand to stop me. He points at the webcam—a silent reminder of our mission. I come back to myself, remembering the script. There will be plenty of time to play. But first thing's first. I wink at Wes/Matt with Amber's long-lashed eye and slip back into my spot in front of the computer.

"What am *I* doing?" Amber asks in the bad porn acting voice that I manipulate. "Why, stepbrother, I'm just sitting here, waiting for you."

"But ours is a forbidden love," Wes, as Matt, replies. He walks over to Amber and kneels next to her, making sure he's fully in the frame of the webcam. "We mustn't."

"Oh, but we must," porno Amber says. Then Wes and I, as Matt and Amber, proceed to make out.

When we hatched the plan, I admit I was curious to know what it would feel like to kiss my boyfriend through the mouth of someone else. I mean, it isn't every day you get the opportunity to do something so randomly weird. I expected it to be funny, or trippy, or hot. But it isn't. At all. Maybe because it's Amber, who I currently loathe, or the fact that I'm not the least bit attracted to Matt. Or maybe it's because this, more than the hair cutting or the Facebook exposé, feels a little too much like a violation. After a few moments, I start to feel gross. I try to pull away, but Wes stays with me, pressing Matt's mouth deeper and harder onto mine.

I play along for another tongue twist or two, until finally, I can't take it. I slam the laptop shut and shove Wes off.

"What was that?" he asks, wiping saliva from Matt's mouth.

"That was gross," I reply, folding Amber's arms across her chest.

"It wasn't meant to be fun," Wes says, rolling his eyes. "It was meant to be effective. Let's make sure the webcam was working."

"It was," I say coolly. The itching scalp returns.

"Then we should know by homeroom if incest is best!" He laughs, and Matt's voice cracks.

I duck out from under his arm and throw Amber onto her bed.

"Come on now," he says. "We're only doing what we agreed to. This is about justice. Remember Amber recorded Gigi kicking your ass in the bathroom and then Snapchatted it. And what about that poor Jenny girl you mentioned? Doesn't she deserve to be avenged? You were the one who thought making Amber cheat on her new boyfriend would offer that justice. But if you're having second thoughts—"

"I'm not," I snap, partly from frustration with Wes, partly from the hivey burn that's traveling across my body. "I just...it feels wrong."

"Of course it does!" Wes says. "Look at these two. There's nothing titillating about getting it on with either of them. That said," he adds, flashing that knee-weakening smile, "I like kissing you in any form."

Wes puts Matt's hand on Amber's leg. "Try this for me. Close your eyes." His fingertips gently caress my lids shut. "And hear my voice," he says in a whisper so soft that Matt's squeaking frog-like tones disappear, and I can imagine it's Wes, body and soul, beside me. When his lips find mine, I'm no longer Amber kissing Matt, but Sarah hungering for Wes.

I sense his body, hovering above mine like we're locked in synchronous orbit, as it guides me back onto the bed until I am lying flat underneath him. I gasp quietly as his weight presses against me, and I wrap my legs around his thighs. We push our pajamaed bodies together, a desperate attempt at fusion, not on Amber's bed, but in the void of the subconscious that defies space and, for a period of no determination, eradicates time.

I taste him, hear his sighs, feel his breath. I forget that it's not him I'm touching, and in a moment of blissful amnesia, I open my eyes.

Matt's face floats above me.

I push him off and stumble out of bed. I shake my head,

my hands, wringing my sin out of me. And that's when I see it—the computer is open, and the camera light is on.

I look at Wes, stunned. Matt stares back at me blankly and shrugs. The crackling buzz returns, and I feel Amber's dinner erupt inside me. I run to her bathroom to puke it up. When I'm done emptying her stomach, I need to escape. I hit my head on the doorframe, hard.

. . . .

I stand above Amber's hollow body as she stretches and sighs, dazed from my attack.

I hear the grunts of the Burners, who have been waiting, as they close in behind me.

I am still.

I welcome them.

I don't know how to run from this.

chapter nineteen

....

Once again, I've awoken from the Burner's embrace frozen inside my own body, my eyelids only half shut. Though I'm in my own bed and there's no threat of Josh or Gigi to terrorize me or of Wes to betray me, I'm scared nonetheless.

It's hard to fully express how total immobility messes with you. How it feels, physically, mentally, to literally find yourself unable to lift a finger or form a word. You feel helpless when you can't call out, frightened when you realize how exposed your body is, panicked when your brain instructs your head to turn but the impulse is ignored. More than anything though, you feel raging frustration. It is the subtext of every other emotion. Because what's happening makes absolutely no sense to your fully functioning brain, which keeps thinking it can reason its way into one little twitch.

But even with the lingering anxiety and physical trauma, there is one thing worse—being trapped with your own thoughts. I keep seeing Matt's face approaching mine, imagine his blank, possessed eyes, smell his hot, wet breath, taste his tongue in my mouth. I try to tell myself it's Wes I was kissing, to rationalize the event. But I can't. It's Matt's body I've done things to that he didn't okay, to say nothing of Amber. I think of myself lying helpless on the bed at the clinic as Josh and Gigi did their worst. Am I the same as them? The thought makes my stomach turn.

But what really makes me want to puke is that I'd recognized this in the moment and stopped myself, only to give back into temptation the second Wes put up a fight. Am I one of those yes girlfriends? Does he have that much control over me?

Wes. The boy who has been used and exploited since he was a child, who needs my love and support more than words can explain, who knows and understands me in a way that literally no one else can, is now also the boy who went behind my back the moment I disagreed with him. And there's something else, something in his attitude about our revenge plans that scares me more than I want to admit. The image of Amber's computer, open and camera on, plays on repeat in my mind. Aren't he and I in this together? Isn't there finally someone on my side? Have I been wrong about him? About all this?

Despite having nothing to do but think, by the time the paralysis wears off late Saturday morning (the extra Dexid prolonging my frozen state), I've gotten nowhere. The only thing I'm sure of is that Wes went way over the line of acceptable boyfriend and human behavior last night, and the fight we're going to have isn't going to be pretty. He'll have to start playing by my rules, or he's out. And it's high time I establish some rules for myself. Like not letting a boy seduce me into delinquency.

I've got no plans to see him until later tonight thanks to a prearranged mother-daughter shopping trip and a dinner date with Tessa, and I'm cool with that. A little space sounds like a good thing right about now. So I decide to turn my phone to silent.

The shopping trip ends up being exactly the comedown I need. It's even fun in a totally normal-life kind of way. Because Mom's so excited about the positive effect the Dexid has on my nighttime habits, she's not only ready for some serious retail celebration but, for the first time in ages, our conversation doesn't linger on sleep. (Save for her excitement that I slept until noon like a regular teenager. Little does she know.) We chat about clothing and movie stars, about college trips and boys. Though I'm not intentionally hiding Wes from her, I know that if I mention him now—specifically where we met—our fun-time, normal-girl's day out will be toast.

By the time we get home, I've only got a few minutes to decide which newly purchased outfit to wear before Tessa picks me up for dinner. Meaning there's no time to confront the multiple texts and calls from Wes that I've ignored. My day of normal has been really nice, and I like the idea of continuing it with fried food and my BFF.

It's nearly eight o'clock when Tessa and I arrive at the Alp, a greasy Greek diner that's everyone's favorite. I'm looking forward to the same easy chitchat that Mom gifted me earlier in the day, but best friends are never as content as parents to keep it superficial.

"So, is Wes the man of your dreams or what?" Tessa asks over cheese fries.

I nearly choke on my soda. "What the...do you...I don't even..." I stammer.

Tessa laughs. "Relax, Sarah. You're not in trouble." A deep thought passes over her face, turning the corners of her mouth down. "Are you?"

"No," I say, laughing myself. But Tessa's frown lingers. "Why do you ask?"

"I don't know. It's just... Listen, I totally don't blame you."

"Blame me for what?" I ask. The tickle of defensiveness straightens my spine.

"Well, not blame..." She searches for words that have been rehearsed.

"Tessa? What's going on?"

She shifts in her seat and leans in. "Okay, I'm just going to lay it out there. You're not acting like yourself, Sar. You're preoccupied. You're cutting class. This thing with Wes is new, and it's yours, and with everything that's been going on lately, I'm glad there's something fun in your life." She pauses, but only to catch her breath. "But you've gone from zero to sixty with this guy, and I don't know if he's really who you should be spending your time with. We already know he's got a shady history at the other schools he's gone to."

"You don't know the whole story," I interject. "Wes has been through a lot. It's not easy for him to let people in." Even though I've got my own issues with my boyfriend, I don't like anyone else trashing him.

"Maybe, but it's not like he's making much of an effort here either. I mean, he was crazy rude to Gigi on his first day."

My mouth falls open. "Gigi? Who'd just slapped me?"

"Gigi, who he had never met before," she rebuffs. "I get defending someone's honor, but at that point, he didn't know either of you. You have to admit it was a little weird."

"As I recall, you thought it was pretty awesome," I say. "And yeah, I may have skipped a few classes, but seriously? I think I'm entitled. Do you have any idea what things have been like?"

"Not really, no," she says coolly. "You've been too busy canoodling with lover boy to even IM me."

Tessa crosses her arms and waits for my response. Part of me understands that she's telling me she feels shut out because she wants me to know that she's here for me; that she only wants to be the friend and confidant she's always been; that she's even saying things about Wes that I've begun to realize on my own. So I should try to explain that, no matter his faults, Wes is the first and only person who actually gets me, and that's the most comfort I've probably had since I was ten. I should tamp down my temper and react to what she's saying. Instead, I embrace the way in which she says it and throw her words back in her face.

"Oh, I'm so sorry I haven't been making you and your neediness my priority," I say.

"My what now?" Tessa shoots back.

"And I'm sorry you're just too above it all to get it," I continue. "It must be tough being the one who never gets called out on anything. Or is it a little boring, always standing outside the center, never committing yourself fully enough to rock the boat?"

Tessa and I have been in very few fights during our decade-long friendship, but when they happen, they're brutal. Neither one of us is good at backing down, and we know each other's weaknesses better than anyone. I prepare for immediate escalation to epic battle, when a ceasefire is called by the little bell attached to the front door of the Alp, ding-a-linging to announce a new arrival.

Amber, surrounded by a clutch of football players and pom girls, enters the diner, laughing loudly and generally stinking up the joint. If they aren't already drunk, they're well on their way. The group takes over one of the larger tables at the back. Amber doesn't acknowledge us as she passes, but for the first time since the slumber party, it doesn't feel malicious. As the jocks clamber to sit next to her, I realize that she's too caught up in being the center of attention to bother being a bitch.

"Huh," a guy's voice says above us. "Didn't see that coming." Wes slides into the booth beside me and attacks me with a passionate, territory-marking kiss. When he's done deep-throating me, he turns to Tessa and holds out his hand. "Hi. We haven't been properly introduced. I'm Wes Nolan."

"Okay," Tessa says evenly, choosing not to comment on the over-the-top PDA. They shake.

Wes digs into our cheese fries while I sit shell-shocked from the kiss, and not in a good way. "What are you girls gabbing about? Must be good for Sarah to ignore my texts." He doesn't look at me as he puts his arm around my shoulder. His muscles are tense, his grip awkward. Between this and the cattle-branding kiss, he's doing me no favors in disproving Tessa's concerns.

My face heats up. I'm mad. Wes is mad. Tessa's mad. Amber's adamantium. In a matter of minutes, my world has been proven flat, and I'm teetering on the edge of oblivion.

"Sorry, it was my fault," Tessa says suddenly. Her voice is friendly but contrite. "I've got some family drama going on, and Sarah was being a pal, talking me through it. We must have lost track. Glad you showed up to join us though. Should we get another order of fries?"

I smile at Tessa, shame faced. Despite her reservations about Wes and her frustration with me, she always has my back.

"Sure," he says and waves down a waitress. After ordering, he returns his attention to Tessa. "So you're supposed to be the girl in the know. What's going on over there? Didn't that chick make a porno or something?"

While I tense, Tessa relaxes. There's nothing like good gossip to perk up my bestie. "She sure did. I mean, it was all over-the-clothes stuff, but yeah, pretty much. Hooked up with her creepola stepbrother while her webcam was on last night."

"No way." Wes's grip softens. If Tessa loves gossip, Wes loves reliving our exploits. I try not to glare at him.

"Truth. I saw it. Total yuck." She sips her Coke. "The thing that's crazy though, Amber doesn't care a bit. The number of times her page has been viewed has increased, like, a billionfold."

"Any publicity is good publicity," Wes says.

"That's what I keep telling Sarah," she agrees, and for a moment, all feels right in the land of best friends and boyfriends. I pick at the cheese fries.

"It started out kind of funny, like a spoof of a Skinemax movie, and then it cut out. When the feed came back a minute or so later, they were going at it hot and heavy. Like, totally into it for realz." Tessa giggles. "I'm so embarrassed even talking about it, but I just couldn't turn it off."

"No judgment here." Wes laughs. "I bet it was hot."

I drop the french fry. Wes doesn't look at me, but there's no way he missed my boiling stare scalding his cheek. Though it's definitely nice to have Tessa and Wes getting along, I'm not sure how much longer I can sit on my rage that he turned the webcam back on when I thought it was just us. Processed cheese bubbles in my stomach, and I resolve to let him have it as soon as Tessa goes for a bathroom break.

"Didn't something new happen with that Gigi girl too?" Wes asks, changing the subject.

Tessa stops laughing, and her mouth contorts into a grimace. "Yeah, but I don't think we need to…"

"Wait, wait. I know I heard something," Wes says, tapping his chin with his index finger as if trying to recall a random bit of information. His nonchalance is as fake as his forgetfulness.

Whatever Wes knows, he's dying for me to hear it almost as much as Tessa wants to avoid me finding out.

As my partner in crime predicted, Gigi's been giving me a wide berth. On the morning of Kiara's fall from grace, she came to school with a new pixie cut, courtesy of some brilliant hairdresser who worked his magic on the mangled mess I'd left, and a decent combination of infinity scarf and foundation to cover up her black eye and stress hives. Though she was doing an admirable job playing off her new look as trendsetting change, when our eyes met across the library stacks during study hall, her fearful expression told me that when Gigi MacDonald looked in the mirror, a cute 'do was not what she saw.

At first, I'd told myself that she was merely getting what she deserved. But as I sit here, watching Amber benefit from our intervention and waiting to hear the latest bit of unsettling Gigi news, my resolve falters. So much has changed in the past week. Not just supernaturally, but in my own way of being. I want to drop my head on the table and lose myself in cheese fries. But first, I need to know what happened to Gigi, only not for the reasons Wes thinks I should.

"Tessa, tell me," I say.

She sighs. "Okay, but I don't want you thinking this is your fault. Gigi's got her own stuff to deal with, and you didn't make her—"

"Tell me," I repeat.

She glares briefly at Wes, who pretends not to notice. "Well, it seems like Gigi's new hairstyle wasn't as much a fashion choice as it was a fashion emergency. For *whatever reason*," she says, her tonal emphasis meant to absolve me of guilt, "Gigi had a bit of a psychotic break and hacked off all her hair in the middle of the night. That was Wednesday. She swears she didn't do it, that she was possessed or something cray like that. I guess she stopped sleeping then, became terrified of the dark and her own bedroom. So her parents checked her into rehab for exhaustion."

"Exhaustion." Wes snorts. "Isn't that what celebs say when they don't want to admit they've got a coke habit?"

Tessa cocks her head to the side, not bothering to hide her distaste for Wes's response. "Listen. I don't know why you have it in for Gigi, but she's our friend."

"She's not Sarah's friend," he shoots back, all lightness gone.

"Yes, she is," Tessa replies slowly, to be sure he's understood. "No matter what's going on between her and Gigi right now, at the end of the day, I know Sarah would never wish this on anyone. Would you?"

I don't respond.

Tessa turns her attention from Wes to look at me. "Would you, Sarah?" she asks again, this time with a little less conviction.

What can I say? Yes, I'm appalled that Gigi's sanity had been pushed so far. I feel genuine concern for her as well as crashing waves of nauseous regret over how she's come to this state. But no matter how much I want to agree with Tessa's assessment of me, there's the irrefutable fact that I am actually the one who did this to her. I try to find words, to say something that will reconcile these two competing parts of me, but I can't. Tessa stares at me until I can do nothing but look away.

It isn't long before she makes an excuse and leaves us for the night.

Once she's gone, I turn to Wes and snap, "What the hell was that?"

He slides to the booth bench opposite me. "What the hell was what?" he asks as he crams some fries into his mouth. He grabs the glass-bottled ketchup and hits the 57 until red goop starts pouring out. I glare, stunned, as he eats.

"Antagonizing Tessa? Making me find out about Gigi's hospitalization like that? Recording our hookup without telling me? Seriously, what is wrong with you?"

Wes puts down the Heinz. "What's wrong with me? What's wrong with you? Gigi's gone the way of the dodo, and Kiara is not only off your back but a cautionary tale. We weren't selling the hookup like we needed to, so I motivated you and took some artistic license. Relax."

"Motivated me? Artistic license?" I bristle. "On what planet is any of this okay?"

Before he can respond, the front door to the Alp jingles again, and Amber's stepbrother Matt storms in, dragging a flush-faced, goth girl behind him. He marches up to Amber's table.

"Tell her, Amber," he says through gritted teeth. He's equal parts pain and fury. "Tell her it wasn't what it looked like."

For a second, Amber looks stunned—as confused and haunted as Matt. But she quickly pulls it together and begins her performance. "Oh, honey," she says in a kewpie-doll voice. "Give yourself some credit." Amber's friends laugh, and the girl who I now understand to be Matt's girlfriend begins to cry. Matt slams his fist on the table, and the laughing stops. Forks clang against plates, and soon, the entire Alp is silent. Amber looks scared, and I realize that the truth that Matt's demanding is way more terrifying to her than the lie she's embraced.

And why wouldn't it be? Wes and I have accomplished exactly what we set out to do—haunt Amber and cram the proof down her throat until she chokes on it. Only Amber doesn't have a gag reflex. As always, she's swallowed down what she doesn't understand, because to think about it is paralyzing. Her rationalization is that she wanted the hookup to happen.

But Matt isn't at the rationalization part yet. He's too desperate to save his relationship. All he wants is Amber to tell the truth. But how can she if she's denying it to herself?

She looks around the Alp, taking in the fact that all eyes are on her. She has a choice. Risk seeming nuts by coming clean that she has no recollection of their hookup, admitting that something crazy is going on, and sparing Matt and his girlfriend the obvious pain she—we—have unintentionally inflicted. Or lie.

For a split second, I wonder if it will be Amber, of all people, to lead us out of the valley of scandal, gossip, misunderstanding, and pettiness that defines our high school existence.

Of course, it's not.

Choosing popular home-wrecker over possessed lunatic, she

straightens herself and smooths her hair. Then she leans forward and says, "We hooked up. Too bad we got caught."

Matt stares at her, his rage momentarily subsiding. "But I...I don't remember," he says, his voice small. A crown of sweat erupts on his forehead. His skin pales, and his cheeks sink in on themselves. He looks like he might faint. Until a blubbering sob breaks the spell.

I watch Matt's girlfriend run from the diner, bawling. I watch Matt stare at Amber until she looks away from him. I watch as he turns and walks out of the Alp, hunched and defeated. And I watch as all my classmates turn into vultures, laughing as they reenact the scene they've just witnessed, tweeting their eyewitness accounts, and snapping selfies to prove they were present when it all went down. Is this really no more than theater to them? A passing diversion for their entertainment?

"Looks like someone needs another lesson," Wes says. "Looks like they all do." As he pops another french fry into his mouth, I throw ten bucks on the table, grab my bag, and walk out.

chapter twenty

"Matt? Matt's…girlfriend?" I call lamely into the dark parking lot beside the diner. I have no idea what I'll say if I actually catch up to either one of them, but I know I can't stay in the Alp watching everyone else not give a crap. Especially when the whole thing is my fault. Amber deserves what she's getting, or at least that's the party line I've chosen. But seeing her stepbrother—a guy I barely know, a guy I have nothing personal against, who I've thrown into this mess without a thought—is tough. And his girlfriend? I try to shake off the image of her splotchy red face streaked with tears, but I can't. I'm no better than Amber with Jenny and Pete. Maybe I'm worse.

The diner door swings open, and a tall figure marches out. Though there's no sign of Matt or his girlfriend, I walk deeper into the parking lot.

Wes catches up to me in less than thirty seconds. He grabs my wrist and spins me to face him. "What was that?" he demands.

I try to pull my arm free, but his hold tightens.

"Let go of my wrist." I spit, yanking my arm to no avail. "You're hurting me!"

Backlit by the Alp's neon sign, the raised, tense shoulders of Wes's silhouette, coupled with the aching in my wrist, tells me he's pretty pissed. Maybe more than pissed. I'm trying to recall the turn and twist move that we learned on self-defense day in health class when his grip loosens enough so I can pull my wrist free. I shelter it against my chest and rub at the pain.

"Sarah, I'm sorry. I didn't mean to." His voice is shaky, unsure. I don't care.

"What the hell, Wes?" I snap.

He abandons his apology and crosses his arms, his imposing figure still towering over me. "What the hell yourself?"

I gape at him. "Me? Me?" I'm so enraged that I can't form a sentence.

"Yes, you," he says. "What was that in there? You left me. Like everyone else."

I blink, and for a moment, I see a ten-year-old boy who's only ever been passed around or discarded by the people in his life. Is this why Wes is mad? Does he think I'm one of them? "I didn't leave you," I say a bit more soberly. "I came to find Matt and his girlfriend."

"What for?"

"To see if they're okay."

We stare at each other in silence. Then Wes laughs. His shoulders relax, and he uncrosses his arms. Just like that, I'm forgiven, and angry Wes is gone. "Oh," he says. "Well, that's nice of you, but what were you going to do after they said, *Nope, we're a mess?*" He adopts a high-pitched voice that I realize is meant to be me and says, "Sorry for the confusion, but Matt was actually possessed by my boyfriend when he kissed Amber, who was possessed by me, so don't sweat it. You two are ace."

"Forget it," I say and walk off. I make it two car lengths before he catches up.

"Oh, come on. Lighten up," he says, matching my stride. I turn to ditch him between two parked cars, but he stays right on me. "No one got hurt."

I stop dead in my tracks. "No one got hurt? Did you not see that poor girl in there? Or that Amber is turning into a queen bitch? What about Gigi being admitted *to a hospital* because of what we did to her? Things are happening that we never intended."

"Technically, *you* were the one who chopped off Gigi's hair," he says as he traces the lapel of my jacket. I smack his hand away. "Joke, joke," he says, mock-frightened. Then he opens his arms to me. "Come here."

I step back until I'm definitely out of his reach, straitjacket my arms across my chest, and turn my face away from him. He exhales loudly.

"Sarah," he says. His voice is sweet and soft. "Sarah, I'm sorry. Come here. Please?"

I don't move.

"I'm sorry I said that. It was stupid."

"Yes, it was," I grumble between clenched teeth.

He takes a step toward me. "And I'm sorry I was mad before. I just don't like seeing you upset. You are not to blame for Gigi's inability to handle the consequences of her bad behavior." Another step. "She needed to be taught a lesson." And another. "And she was. But it is not your fault that she didn't like being told no."

I don't move away when his hands find my arms, and I don't flee as he pulls me closer. I feel terrible about Matt and his girlfriend, but are they acceptable collateral damage? Gigi needed to be knocked down a peg or two; of that I'm pretty sure. But did we go too far? Could we make our little world a better place with something subtler than body snatching? Or is this really what it takes to get results? Everything from scripture to Spider-Man tells me that I'm responsible for my actions, but Wes's words, his touch, the way he speaks, makes me question the very definition of the word *responsibility*. And it's so much easier to believe what he's saying.

I bang my head against his chest, and he wraps his arms around me. "I'm freaked," I say into his jacket. "And you're supposed to be on my side."

"I am on your side," he says.

"It didn't feel like it last night. I thought the webcam was off, and you…"

"I know, I know." He pets the top of my head. "And I'm

sorry. I won't do anything like that again. I shouldn't have tricked you."

"No," I say. "You shouldn't have." I relax a little in his embrace. It's good to feel protected, if not exactly safe.

"But to be honest," he continues, "I sort of couldn't stop myself. I was wired last night. Really buzzing. Every impulse felt like the right thing to do. So I did it without considering anything at all."

I look up at him. "I know exactly what you mean." I think of the throbbing desire I had to escape Amber's itching body and shudder at the memory of the paperweight. Relief spreads over me. It wasn't Wes who betrayed me but a drug-fueled version of him that isn't who he really is. Just like I haven't really been myself either.

"It's the Dexid." I say. "We took too much, and it's making us do bad things. And not just last night. But every night. It's gone too far."

"Shhhh," he says. "No matter how far you go, don't you know that I'll go further just to be with you? I'll stay with you, always. I'll never abandon you. Ever. We're linked in a cosmic way that we're only beginning to understand. And whatever needs to be done, we'll do together. We'll make it right."

"But how?" I ask. "We can't take it back. I thought we'd be finished after Amber, but that didn't exactly work out how we wanted. She's more of a monster now than ever."

"Yeah, we'll need to do something about that," he says thoughtfully. "Maybe humiliation isn't the way to go." He kisses the top of my head. Then, as blasé as if he's throwing out dinner suggestions, he says, "Disfigurement?"

I laugh, but when his matter-of-fact expression remains unchanged, I choke on my own amusement. My eyes widen as if by seeing more of him, I might be able to comprehend what he's just said. I can't. I shove his chest hard, pushing myself backward and out of his embrace. I turn and stalk off.

The front of the parking lot is well lit, but that does nothing to stop Wes once he catches up to me. He grabs my shoulders and spins me to face him. I swing my free arm and manage to make contact with his right bicep, but he absorbs the hit with only a tiny grunt. Then, in a frighteningly focused move that comes way too easily, he pushes my arms down into an X and pins them to my own chest. I kick, but he spins me again so my back is against him, and he spreads his legs, making it harder for me to make contact. My heart thrums in my chest.

"I am not letting you go until you calm down," he hisses in my ear.

"And I am not calming down until you stop being a total psycho!" I yell. "Jesus, you have to get off the Dexid. It's making you a complete dick!"

"How?" he asks. "By allowing me to do what I want, when I want to? It's about time I got some control. I think a little id is good for the soul. Just because you can't handle it doesn't mean I have to go to rehab."

I kick back again, and this time, I catch part of his shin.

He grunts, but my achievement is purely symbolic. His embrace tightens, and I lose my breath.

My pulse quickens. Sweat breaks out across my flesh. I close my eyes and involuntarily imagine a Burner. I'm suddenly there—wrapped in the monster's arms, being held so tightly that I believe my eyes will pop out, that my teeth will fall out, that my eardrums will burst. I feel the terror at knowing once this is over, I'll still be trapped, imprisoned in my own body until some arbitrary clock deems me once again worthy to be the boss of my physical self. I recall all this so vividly that the panic I feel is as real as in my nightmares.

But it's not a nightmare. I'm not asleep. And this is not a Burner holding me but a boy. The boy who says he's my everything yet is trying to squeeze me into nothing. I'm not afraid. I'm furious. It feels good.

I still my body, slow my breathing. I stop fighting him, and as promised, the less I struggle, the looser Wes's grip becomes until finally, he lets go of me.

I can turn around now and smack him or spit in his face and run off. There's an infinite number of ways the moment can go that will keep things between us. No one else needs to get involved. But I'll never know. Because I don't get the chance to make the next move.

Jamie makes it for me.

"Sarah?" my ex says as he emerges from his car. "Are you all right?"

I jump at the growl in Jamie's voice. This is not good. This

fight is between Wes and me alone, and I must defuse this poten-
tially nuclear situation now. All I can think to do is play it cool.
So I walk straight over to Jamie and give him a hug.

"Hey. Yeah, I'm great," I say cheerfully. "How are you?
Headed to the Alp?"

Jamie says nothing, just stares at Wes.

"Where are my manners?" I say. "I bet you two haven't met."

"Nope," Wes replies. He's glaring too.

"Sarah, I think you should come inside," Jamie says. He
holds out his hand to me but keeps his eyes locked on Wes.

Crap.

"Thanks, but we ate with Tessa already. In fact, I kind of
need to get going. My mom wants me in early tonight."

"Good," says Jamie. "I'll drive you."

At this, Wes laughs. "Thanks, pal, but Sarah's got a ride."

No one moves. My good guy ex and unhinged boyfriend
stare each other down. The last thing I need is two testosterone-
happy guys going at it right now. But I have no idea how to stop
this showdown. I open my mouth to say something, anything,
to just talk until I come up with a plan. But before a single sound
escapes, Jamie takes my hand and pulls me toward the stairs of
the Alp.

Wes grabs my other arm and yanks me away from Jamie,
shoving me behind him. Without the slightest pause, Jamie pivots
and swings. The crack of knuckle hitting bone pops in the cool
night air. Wes staggers sideways, landing on the hood of a car.

He licks blood at the corner of his mouth and smiles. It's not unlike the crooked smirk that I once found so enticingly playful. But now there's menace in its curve. Jamie's violence is exactly what Wes has been waiting for. The license to lose his shit. He doesn't want to unleash it on me. He wants me. But in Jamie, all he sees, all he's ever wanted to see, is the unnatural system he's never fit into and is determined to take down. It doesn't matter who Jamie really is—a jock who deserves a beating or a doctor who sees Wes as nothing more than a lab rat. Wes is giddy with self-deputized license.

I throw myself between them.

"Jamie, it's time to go," I say.

"Yes, it is," he agrees and turns toward the Alp.

It takes him a couple of steps before he realizes that I'm not coming with him. He turns back to look at me, and his expression makes my stomach ache. I've known Jamie since we were twelve years old. He was my first love and a true friend. I've known him happy and sad, but I've never seen him look this defeated.

I meet his eyes, but only for a second. Shifting my focus to the shoulder of his letterman jacket, I will myself not to cry. He shoves his hands in his pockets, turns, and walks up the stairs into the Alp. He doesn't look back.

I feel Wes's arms slide around my waist in machismo triumph, and he rests his chin on my shoulder. He squeezes me softly as he breathes in my hair. He needs me, needs us.

But I do not.

"We're done," I say.

He stops breathing.

"We're done when we're done," he replies. "And there's still so much for us to do." He slides his hand under my shirt and runs his finger up my side, but I ignore it.

"I'm not taking the Dexid tonight," I say.

"Yes, you are. You need it," he whispers. His fingers trace the underwire of my bra.

"I'd rather be held down by straps than under your thumb," I reply.

"You seem to like my thumb right now." His fingers switch direction, traveling down my body. I want to shiver, but I don't move a muscle.

"You're a grenade," I say.

"And you're the pin. You wouldn't leave me to my own devices, would you? Who knows what I might do without you." He turns me around to face him. "Make no mistake. I won't let anyone come between us. Not even you."

My breath catches in my throat. I finally, truly understand that he's meant every word he's ever said to me.

And I'm so not cool with that.

Suddenly, everything comes back to me from Mrs. Burke's self-defense lesson. I place my palms on Wes's shoulders. Shift my weight to my back leg. Thrust my front knee up into his groin.

Hard.

In the moment of pained confusion that overwhelms him, I pull myself free and run.

chapter twenty-one

I run home through side alleys and backyards, taking a route that no one who isn't a local would ever dream up. When I arrive at my house, I lock the door and run to my room. I skip the Dexid and have my mom strap me to the bed. I close my eyes and wait for sleep.

It doesn't come.

I lay awake for hours, going over everything that's happened in the past week. Attempted manslaughter, losing my friends, finding my dream guy, inhabiting other people's dreams, inhabiting other people, hurting those people. How have things gotten so out of hand? Is it the extra Dexid we've taken that's messing with our judgment? Should I lay all the blame on Wes and the meds? Can I excuse his behavior because of that little gold pill? Or are Wes and I alone more responsible than I care to admit?

I think Wes is an addict. And so am I. But I'm not sure which new vice in my life I'm the most addicted to. I breathe deep and tell myself to let it all go. Take the night off. I'll deal with that one addiction, Wes, in the morning. He can't get to me without the Dexid in my system. I'm alone. I'm safe. At least for tonight.

I finally begin to nod off around one am. Drifting then dozing, I'm on my way to an uninhabitable sleep when the sound of my window opening jolts me awake. I freeze as the shadow of an imposing male figure crawls from the thick branches of the old oak outside my window into my room. I'm about to scream when said figure waves.

"Jamie, what are you doing?" I whisper furiously. "My mother's down the hall. You almost gave me a heart attack!"

He moves to the edge of my bed. "I had to come check on you," he says. "After the parking lot and that jackass. I needed to know you were all right."

"Okay, fine," I say. "But first, a little help please?" I jiggle my wrists and ankles against my restraints. Jamie unbuckles each one then sits opposite me on my bed.

"I'm all right," I say finally. "Tonight was not so good. Things with me and Wes are..." I pause, searching for the right word.

"Complicated?" he asks.

I snort. "You could say that. We just had a fight about some stuff we're not really seeing eye to eye on right now."

His jaw clenches, and a muscle pulses in the hollow of his cheek. "You going to break up with him?"

I sigh. "If only it were that simple. Honestly? I don't know what to do. He really freaked me out tonight but we have a... connection. I don't think I can just walk away."

"Sure you can," Jamie says. "You put one foot in front of the other and leave. Plenty of others have done it before."

His fisted knuckles palpitate, and his voice burns like acid. Jamie may be a friend, but he's a former boyfriend too—and probably not the best choice for a heart to heart about Wes. Time to change the subject.

"Listen," I say. "I appreciate you checking on me. Truly. But I'm okay. And you have to go. Remember the last time my mom caught you in my bedroom?" I smile, recalling the time we got busted during a PG-13 headed for R-rated hookup.

The memory makes me blush. But when I look back at Jamie, he's frowning.

"I'm sorry," I say. "I shouldn't have brought up when we were together."

"Want to know the truth?" He puts his hand on my naked thigh just below where my pajama shorts cut off. "I wish you'd think about those times more often."

I stare at Jamie. I'm shocked by his boldness but, if I'm being honest, not all that surprised. Seeing me with Wes can't be easy for him, and in some ways, it's not easy for me. It isn't like I stopped liking Jamie when we broke up. I dumped him because I was trying to protect him. And maybe because I told myself he was too good for me. Jamie is the stable guy, the one who's always been there.

"But I'm with…"

He puts his finger to my lips and leans forward.

When Jamie looks at me, he sees the normal girl who I used to so desperately want to be. The me I should probably get back to. And maybe I can with him by my side, balancing my crazy— unlike Wes, who exponentially multiplies it. What if Jamie is my cure? He's strong, kind, and he still wants me.

I don't move as he replaces his finger with his mouth. And when his lips part, I plunge, searching for the past, the familiar, for a homing beacon to guide me back to the real Sarah and away from the Bonnie I've become to Wes's Clyde.

But the kiss is the opposite of comfort. It cuts any ties I have left to normalcy. It's awkward, strange, foreign, wrong. It's the furthest thing from the sweet, romantic kisses Jamie once gave me.

Because the person I'm kissing isn't Jamie. It's Wes.

I ricochet backward, slamming against the headboard. I wipe my mouth violently with the back of my hand.

"Psycho," I hiss.

"Slut," Wes says from within Jamie.

"Get out of him," I demand. "Get out of him right now."

"Or what?" he asks. He places Jamie's hands behind his head and leans casually against them. "Though I hate to admit it, your ex here is quite the specimen, Sarah. I can see why you want him."

"I don't want him!" I scream-whisper. "You just showed up at the right time. I'm about fifty-two cards short of a full deck right now, and your mind games aren't helping."

Jamie's face is cold, stony. Wes says nothing.

"What?" I demand. "Do you want me to say I'm sorry? To apologize for turning to Jamie after what you pulled in Amber's dream and your schizo reality break at the Alp? I might not be employee of the month in the girlfriend department, but you're batting a thousand at the psychopath games. Honestly, Wes, this is no way to have a relationship."

"I warned you there would be consequences," he says.

"Oh, right," I snarl, rolling my eyes. "Well, you've exposed me for the unfaithful slut I am by throwing me into the arms of someone else. Well done! Congrats!"

Wes's crooked smile warps Jamie's face. "That's not the consequence, Sarah. That was just the setup."

I look at him, incredulous and, at first, not understanding.

Then my eyes widen in panic. "Wes, how much Dexid did you take?" No reply. "Oh God, please," I plead, the fury and the fight totally gone. "This has nothing to do with Jamie. Don't do anything stupid."

Wes jumps to Jamie's feet. "Oh, I think I can do just about anything I want to. I mean, isn't that the beauty of this whole thing? I am in complete control of this body, and I can do whatever I want with or to it. It's up to me. Not him, not you—me."

His body is tense, humming. He paces the room like a captive tiger patrolling the perimeter of his cage. "What if I drink lover boy blind and then go for a drive? That'd be interesting. Or maybe I'll just grab a hammer and smash his throwing hand."

Wes stops and looks at me. Then he pounces on the bed. I scramble backward, but he pins me down as his body straddles mine. "Or maybe I'll have him do the things to you that you're so clearly itching for."

He puts his hand on my throat and tightens just enough to let me know things can still get much worse. "Sarah," he says wistfully. "We could have been so great together. I mean, you'd have thought we were destined, right? That we belonged together, two halves of a single whole." He lowers his voice as if telling me a secret. "You know, I'd always sensed a part of me was missing. I thought I'd found it when I met you." With a snarl of disgust, he releases his grip and pushes himself off me. "Oops, my bad."

Standing, he walks toward the window. "Now if you'll excuse me, I'm going to see what it's really like to be Captain America. Remember, whatever happens to Jamie is your fault."

Panic cyclones through my body. I have to stop him from hurting Jamie, but how? Reasoning with him isn't an option, and fighting him is clearly out. Physically, Wes is a formidable enough foe in his own body, but in Jamie's, I don't stand a chance. Which is why he doesn't expect an attack.

I move on desperate instinct. Reaching behind my mattress, I yank the plug from the wall, grab my bedside lamp, and run full force at my possessed ex. Before he can react, I smash the lamp over his head.

Jamie collapses on the floor, unconscious but Wes-free. I try to drag him to my bed, to tie him up with my restraints before Wes has the chance to invade his body again, but there's no way I can move two hundred pounds of dead weight. So I do the only thing that comes to mind. I race to my bathroom and throw open the medicine cabinet. I grab a Dexid, swallow it dry, and pray for sleep.

Within moments, my eyelids…

shut…

and…

I am in the station's lower tunnels. I run through the maze of halls and arches like I'm following a map, until I come to a ramp that leads to an idling train—and any number of doors that Wes could have gone through.

Which dream is Jamie's? How do I find him?

I have no idea, no sense of where he could be. I feel lost again, alone. I may see the station, but I might as well be in the dark, groping around blind. Like my first night on Dexid when I fell out of the train. When I was falling in the void, plummeting into nothingness.

Until I thought of Tessa.

My heart skips. I thought of Tessa, and I found her. And when we dosed Gigi and Amber and Kiara, I found them too.

And Wes.

I think of his words, of what he said. That he was alone until I found him.

Okay, Lover Boy, *I think.* Show yourself.

I close my eyes and imagine him. His anger and manipulations, his superior attitude, and his hatred of Jamie.

I open my eyes. Nothing. Nothing has changed except for how thoroughly pissed off I am. I shake it off and try again.

This time, I picture Wes as I first saw him in the station. I see his eyes, bright and alive, anxious but excited. I see his half-cocked grin inviting me to play. I feel his hand, firm and sure, guiding me. His embrace protecting me. His breath reviving me.

My body lightens... My feet skim the ground... The hum of the idling train fades into a white noise lullaby... I open my eyes, and the colors of the train have muted, save for one door that glows brighter than all the rest.

Bingo.

I go to it.

And step inside.

Jamie's dreamscape is simple. A cavernous room with vaulted ceilings, polished wood floors, nothing but old pews lining the outer walls. And two guys facing off in its center. Jamie wobbles where he stands, his head in his hands as though coming to with a wicked hangover after an eventful night he'll never remember. Wes is on all fours a few yards away, struggling to his feet after his violent expulsion from Jamie. He's dazed but coming around quickly. I don't have much time to stop him, but I think I've got a chance.

Until...

A low growl rumbles behind me.

A Burner looms in the doorway.

I am not as quick on my feet as I need to be, and the beast comes up faster than I can take off. I'm sure I am toast. But then it sidesteps me and continues on.

It's not after me. It wants to stop Wes.

But Wes doesn't even realize the Burner's there. He's completely focused on Jamie, and he's closer to the dreamer than anyone. As the Burner charges, Wes tries to leap the last few yards to jump into Jamie's

*body, but he trips over his own feet and wipes out just as the Burner
reaches them.*

The monster is going too fast.

It can't stop itself.

It flies over a prone Wes and in a single

WHOOSH

   the Burner rips into Jamie.

*Jamie absorbs the demon, swallows this nightmare whole. His body
goes rigid. Then he opens his mouth and howls.*

The Burner is possessing Jamie.

*Have I ever seen this before? No. The Burners are always careful to
avoid the dreamers. They've never touched me or Wes when we're inside
one. Maybe they're not supposed to touch them. Because they shadow
them just like we do. Only while Wes and I seem to understand enough
of what's going on to control the dreamer when we're inside one, the
Burners do not.*

*The monster inside Jamie thrashes about, panicked, ping-ponging
off unseen objects. He looks like Frankenstein's monster confronted with
fire. I flinch with every ricochet, imagining the bedposts, desks, and walls
he is crashing into in my bedroom.*

*I determine to expel the Burner, like how I pushed Wes out of
Gigi when I jumped into her in her dream, praying that the rules that
apply to me and Wes also apply to the Burner. But as I near Jamie's
possessed body, he trips over something invisible to me and all too real
in the waking world. He stumbles backward, and in a pantomime I will
see forever, he falls.*

Instead of hitting the chapel floor, Jamie's body rises off the ground.

As he levitates in this dream, he falls elsewhere. His legs flail. His arms grasp, but there is nothing in any reality to grab hold of.

Finally, he crashes—hard—onto the chapel floor.

There is a loud snap.

Jamie, and the Burner inside him, disappear.

. . . .

The buzzing of my iPhone is the first sound I register. It's morning, and for a second, I have that peaceful sense of promise that the start of a new day brings. Then I hear idling vehicles and raised voices outside my window, and the events of the night before come flooding back. I shoot up in my bed and open my eyes to blinding daylight. Someone grabs my arms.

"Shhh, shhh," my mother says as her face comes into focus. Her eyes are bloodshot and red-rimmed.

"Mom? What happened?" I look at my open window and the yellow police tape crossing it. I reach for my nightstand and grab my cell. I've missed over a dozen calls and texts from Tessa.

"Honey," my mom says as she takes the phone from me. "I need you to listen to me. There's been an accident. Jamie was trying to sneak into your room last night, and he must have lost his footing or something because..." She trails off as she catches sight of the broken lamp on the floor.

"Sarah, when did you take a Dexid? I've been trying to wake you for hours. It was before Jamie fell, right? Otherwise, you'd have heard—"

"Mommy," I say. "Tell me what happened to Jamie."

Tears spill down my mother's face. "Oh, Sarah. Jamie fell out of your window. He broke his back."

chapter twenty-two

I've been known to call many things tragic, from a lost lip gloss to a broken heart. But to watch, helpless, as someone you care for loses the life he's always known in an instant? That puts everything else in embarrassing perspective. I spend the day alternating between two equally destructive states: crying about what's happened to Jamie and over the waking nightmare that Wes has turned out to be, and fighting with my mother to let me go to the hospital where Jamie's in surgery. After hours of trying to dissuade me from the latter, she finally comes out with the harshest but only effective argument: The last person Jamie's distraught parents need to see right now is the girl whose window their son fell out of. I shut up after that.

Around four p.m., Tessa texts me that the student council

and pom squad have scheduled a vigil on campus for tonight. I ask my mother if I can attend (or am I the last person the pom squad needs to see too?) and she gives me the okay. Tessa picks me up right after dinner, and before we've made it out of the driveway, we're both crying.

"I'm so sorry," I say between sobs. "I never want to fight with you."

"Me neither," she agrees, her voice hoarse. We hug over the gearshift and don't let go as we cry some more. "This thing with Jamie just reminds me that anything can happen any time. And I don't want to be in a stupid fight with you if it does. We're here for each other no matter what. Right?"

"Always," I say.

Tessa gives me a final squeeze before extricating herself from my embrace. "I just can't make sense of it," she says as she reverses out of my driveway. "I mean, I know that the police think he was sneaking into your room from the window and slipped, but it's just so weird. He's done that climb, like, a hundred times. If I was going to worry about anyone falling out of your window in the middle of the night, it'd be you during an episode. Not Jamie. I don't get it."

I cringe. Tessa's absolutely right. Jamie's injury wasn't an accident. It was a brutal attack. And it's because of me that it happened. All day, my hands have been in a permanent white-knuckled state, my body constantly tense, waiting for Wes, the boogeyman, to jump out of the shadows. I'm unraveling, and I need help sorting through everything. But how and with whom?

Can I tell Tessa? Where would I start? How do I explain everything that's happened? And what will she say once she knows all the terrible things I've done?

"Tessa," I say, my knees twitching.

"What?"

"There's some stuff I need to tell you."

"About Wes," she states more than asks.

I nod. "I realize now is not the best time."

"Any time is fine, Sar," she says, glancing over at me. "I know something's not right. And whenever you want to tell me about it, I'm here."

"Good. Because I think I need to talk. A lot." I take a deep breath and close my eyes as she turns the corner onto campus. "There's something you need to know about—"

"Oh my God. Sarah, look."

I open my eyes as we pull into the visitor's parking lot. My confession stops. Hundreds of people flood the football field. Drama geeks are handing out candles as cheerleaders sing hymns. The popular, the disenfranchised, the stoners, the brainiacs—they're all here. There's a weeping freshman girl who I doubt Jamie has ever even spoken to being consoled by her friends near the bleachers. And on the field itself, you can barely see an inch of grass. All I can really see, for what feels like miles in front of me, is a gently rippling wave of warm, glowing lights held by friends, family, acquaintances who are all here to mourn what's happened to Jamie.

It's beautiful.

And it pisses me off.

Who are these people coopting Jamie's tragedy for their own emotional growth spurts? Suddenly, they care enough to stand next to their enemies and cry on the shoulders of strangers? They're acting like the decent people they should always be. But it's taken something really awful happening to someone really good for them to bother.

Then I chastise myself for this ungracious response. Because honestly, who am I to judge? Isn't this break from their regularly scheduled apathy way less offensive than the guerilla warfare I've been waging? Sure, the fact that they might not have cared as much had this happened to some cosplay enthusiast makes my stomach turn almost as much as the #standwithjamie hashtag does, but they aren't the ones seeking out offenders and doling out punishment. That's me. At least these hypocrites have the decency not to paralyze anyone.

I'm feeling sick to my stomach, literally made ill by the bleak conclusions about the human condition that are infecting my brain, and wondering if this is more evidence of Wes's influence or my own sorry outlook (and which is worse?). I turn to Tessa to say as much, to spill everything, to make someone else sort through all the crazy going on in my head, when I see that she's smiling with tears rolling down her face.

"Isn't this amazing?" she asks.

I shelve my confession, smile back, and say, "Yeah." I squeeze her hand. Tessa's done so much for me. She's never blinked at my disorder, never wavered when I became persona non grata. I owe it to her to keep her out of this mess. I'll protect her, like I didn't protect Jamie.

As soon as we get out of the car, a girl walks up to us holding candles. She hands one to Tessa and turns to me. She's a short, blond pom girl with a sweet, round face. Her dimpled smile is just the right balance of friendly and solemn. But it curves downward into an accusing scowl the instant she registers who I am. She yanks the candle in her outstretched arm back, and I grasp air.

"What are you doing here?" she spits.

"Excuse you?" Tessa says.

"She heard me," Dimples replies with all the righteous indignation of the outwardly blameless. "This event is for people who want to mourn what happened to Jamie, not for those who caused it."

My first impulse is to smack those dimples right off this brat's face. My second? To start plotting how to slip her some Dexid. I shudder at how quickly my thirst for revenge overwhelms my brain, and all the fight in me dries up.

"It's okay. I'll go," I say.

"The hell you will," Tessa snaps. She steps to Dimples, and I begin to sweat. Being the cause of a fight at Jamie's vigil is not a good idea. I stand there, useless, having no clue how to defuse the situation, just waiting to find myself in the aftermath of yet another mess, when a shock of orange hair and a pair of broken glasses shuffles up to save the day.

"Ladies," Grady says. "I think we're all a little upset, but there's no need to take it out on each other. Especially not tonight. Is there?"

Tessa continues to glare at Dimples but takes a step back. When the pom girl doesn't move, Grady shoves his hands deep into his pockets and sighs. "Lindsay," he says calmly. "Back off and give Sarah a candle, or I'll replace the pom squad's Adderall supply with Xanax just in time for state's."

Lindsay's mouth falls open, but she says nothing. She shoots me an icy glare and drops the unlit candle at my feet before stomping off.

"Thanks, Grady," I say as I pick up the candle.

"I'd say 'anytime,' but I'm not sure if I can keep up with all the people you've pissed off lately," he replies, and I manage a real smile.

"Well, aren't you two just the cutest little odd couple? How long has this been happening?" Tessa asks as she looks from me to Grady.

He shrugs, and she laughs. Even though what he's said is depressingly true, I relax just a little as Tessa links her arm through mine and motions for Grady to join us on the field.

As we weave through the crowd, I ask, "Any updates from the hospital?" Though Mom was probably right about how Jamie's parents would've reacted to my presence, I'm sure nothing could have kept Meat away from his best friend's bedside.

"Word is the surgery went okay," Grady offers. "But Mrs. Washington pretty much cried the whole time Jamie was in the OR."

I bite the inside of my cheek to stop my own tears at that.

"Do they have any more ideas about what happened?" Tessa asks. "I just can't believe he missed the jump."

"Nope," Grady says. "But my brother did say some cop was asking about drugs. Sent Mr. Washington into a rage."

"Drugs?" Tessa gasps. "I mean come on. That's ridiculous. Jamie?" She laughs with no mirth, and I barely stifle a shudder.

"Pretty standard cop question in a situation like this, I'd guess," Grady replies dispassionately. He glances at me over the top of his glasses. "Then again, you never really know about people, do you? They can surprise you."

As Tessa launches into a lecture about Jamie's clean living and Grady's skewed worldview, I notice he's keeping an eye on me. Could he know something? But how? And what? What could he even understand? Does he think I'm somehow responsible for what happened to Jamie? Would he be wrong?

We stop at an open pocket in the crowd from which we can just see the makeshift stage at the far end of the visiting team bleachers. The glee club is finishing up a somber rendition of "Stand by Me" as we all light our candles off a friendly hippy chick sporting a flowery dress and jeans ensemble.

Trisha Goldmark gets on the mic to announce that a bake sale to raise money for Jamie's hospital bills is happening by the south bleachers. Then she informs the owner of a blue Honda Odyssey that his lights are on before finally introducing Reverend Hiller, the local minister from the Unitarian Church where Jamie's family attends services. My mom considers herself a student of all religions, so we've done brief stints just about everywhere—from Shabbat service at Temple Beth El to Quaker meeting—but nothing ever really stuck. Still, as the reverend asks everyone assembled to take a step closer to their neighbor and move toward the stage, I feel a desperate hope that whatever he's going to say might offer a little bit of clarity in all this fog.

As the crowd shuffles forward, filling in the gaps, Tessa and I are separated. I can still see her with Grady, about three people removed from me. She's hanging on Reverend Hiller's every word, joining him in the Lord's Prayer in full voice. My lips start to move too as I recall what I can from a couple of Sunday school visits, and I begin to get swept up in the moment. Can all these voices united in love and prayer for Jamie actually make a difference? I so want to believe in something other than the havoc Wes and I have wreaked.

I know I can't go back, but I can stop doing all the terrible things I'm capable of. Just because you own a loaded gun doesn't mean you need to pull the trigger, right? Of course, I did try to stop, to stay away from Wes, and where did it get me? Jamie is in the hospital, Wes is still out there, and I have absolutely no idea what to do.

I listen to the crowd chant *amen* and decide to try the only thing I haven't yet—pray. As Reverend Hiller asks the crowd to bow their heads in a moment of silent reflection, I, along with everyone around me, comply.

The shared silence of hundreds of people is exceptionally

moving. For the first time in days, I feel peace. It's so striking that I become overwhelmed, unaccustomed as I am to any sense of calm. I don't want to lose this feeling, but I need more air in my lungs, so I lift my head, just for a moment. And that's when I see him. The only person not looking down. The only person staring straight at me.

Wes leans against the bleachers where the bake sale is set up. He holds a cookie in the air and waves.

I weave through the crowd and reach him just as Reverend Hiller lifts his head and the elementary school's small chorus begins to sing.

"Cookie?" Wes asks.

I knock it out of his hand.

"Hey," a girl behind the table says. "You need to pay for that."

Wes smiles at me. "Christa here is helping raise money to get Jimmy a new back. Who wouldn't want to contribute to that?"

The lovestruck underclassman blushes. "His name is Jamie, Wes," she somehow whispers and giggles at the same time. Wes face-palms his forehead, and Christa squeaks. I want to punch them both, but I go for my wallet instead.

"Get the cookies," Wes suggests as he winks at Christa. "They're delish."

"Brownie bites," I snap.

"That'll be four dollars," Christa says as she hands me a ziplock bag of a dozen or so chocolate treats.

I throw her a five and grab Wes by the wrist. To Christa's chagrin, I pull him away from the bake sale to the far end of the bleachers, out of earshot if not eyesight of the crowd. I can still make a run for it if I need to.

"Who knew this was what people needed to come together?" Wes says, surveying the crowd. "Can't imagine what they'd do if this happened to more than just one dumb jock."

I lunge at him, but he grabs my arm and stops me from making hard contact.

"No, no," he says. "You don't want to make a scene."

"You think I care?" I hiss.

"More than anything," he replies. "But we'll get to that. First, I want to give you one last chance. So we had a fight. A bad one. But if you agree to get back with the program, I'll give you my full forgiveness, and we can start over."

My cold sweat turns red hot. "Do you have brain damage? After what you did to Jamie?" I whisper furiously. "Screw you." I pull against him, but he tightens his fingers to the point of bruising us both.

"Haven't we been here already? Calm down, and I'll let you go. Fight me again, and I'll dose everyone in a fifty-foot radius and throw them to the Burners."

I look at the defenseless people around me, counting Tessa and Grady in that lot. Despite the fact that all I want to do is run, to escape from this nightmare, I understand now that I can't walk away. I've got no clue what to do next, but I know I won't figure it out with Wes slowly crushing me.

"Fine," I say. I stop pulling against him, and he lets go. I follow him under the bleachers. "This is far enough."

"Come on. Take a walk with me," he purrs.

"Not a chance," I reply and fold my arms.

Grin becomes glower. He holds out his hand. "Come or I'll—"

"You'll what?" I snap, what little patience I have finally gone. "Time for another threat? Is this the only way you can get a girl to be alone with you now? You're pathetic."

He drops the hand, and I can tell I've hit a nerve.

"Relationship problems?" I continue. "Try seducing your girlfriend by pretending to be someone else. Not working? How about pummeling her ex-boyfriend until he ends up in the hospital? Still not enough? Why not follow her around like a sad little—"

"I didn't follow you here," he says, but I ignore him.

"You nearly kill Jamie, and then you show up at his vigil and think what? Flash her a smile, she'll ride off into the sunset with you? You're delusional." I spit the words at him. "This is real life with real people. And I happen to like a lot of them. So no, I'm not going anywhere with you. I'm staying here, with my friends, and my frenemies, and the people who annoy the hell out of me, because that's what you do. You don't try to control the world. You just deal with it."

Wes stares at me for a long time. The silence begs for a reply, but I won't blink first. Finally, he nods. "You know, I had our whole reconciliation planned out. Even after all your denials and betrayals, I thought, but she's my other half. We balance each other. I push you to be cool with who you really are, and you remind me what's real, what matters."

He steps in closer. I can feel the warmth of his body through the chilly air between us. "Believe it or not, Sarah, you matter to me." The corner of his mouth curls up. "I think you're amazing. I really do. I want to see you fly. I want to help you fly. So I'll ask you one last time: why can't we just do this? Together."

His hand moves to my hip, but for the first time, there's no warm rush of blood to my skin where his fingers touch. Just cold.

I push him off. "Because there's no way to use this power without abusing it. Do you just not get it? Every time we enter someone's dreams, we're trespassing. Even if we do nothing, we're going into someone's mind uninvited. It's the sci-fi version of hacking the cloud for naked photos."

His lips return to a tight, straight line. He rolls his eyes. "Ugh. Spare me this moral dilemma again. Fine, whatever. You're out. I can take a hint." He takes a step back, cracks his neck, and rolls his shoulders, like a fighter loosening up before a bout. "But since this sounds like good-bye, I want to tell you something." He puts a hand to his heart. "I honestly didn't know the Burners could enter the dreamer. I wanted to screw with you and with Jamie, but I had no idea it was going to end that way."

I side-eye him and wonder if this could possibly be the truth. Even after everything, I would love to believe him, to think that he planned to give me a scare and then climb back out the window and put Jamie, unharmed, back into his bed.

"I thought…I still think the Burners are there to counteract us and what we can do. But now"—his eyes flicker—"thanks to Captain Wonderful, we know how to protect ourselves from them. And that ain't bad news."

"What?" I ask. "What do you mean protect ourselves?"

Wes bows his head and speaks slowly, as if to a child. "Burners are supposed to protect the dreamers. From us. But they can't enter a dreamer, like Jamie, without having a full-on fit. That's why when we're inside a dreamer, the Burner won't touch us. Did you notice that the Burner who fell into Jamie disappeared when Jamie did? If we can trap the Burners in dreamers, they can't come back to get us. We're free."

Heat rages through my body as I comprehend the meaning of his words. "You want to use our classmates as pest control?"

"If it keeps the monsters away from me, why the hell not?"

I kick myself for my momentary misguided softness and shake my head. "Because you can just stop, Wes. You have to stop! We don't have to take the Dexid. We don't have to put anyone in danger." I look into his eyes, normally sparkling wild, now dark and cold. "But you don't want to, do you? You said it yourself: the lows are sub-basement, but the highs are miles above the Empire State. And that high is worth more than anything or anyone else. Including me."

He grunts. "Spare me your intervention, Sarah. Just because you're cool with mediocrity doesn't mean you can proselytize to me." His mouth snarls in disgust. "You have so much potential. But what a waste you've turned out to be. That train station, and everything that happens in it, is one of two realities in which we live. It's not a choice; there is no other option. You've been given a gift, and you just want to pitch it. Sure. Whatever. But me? I'm going to rule the world. I'm going to learn how to control every inch of dreamland, and I will drug every person here, follow them into their nightmares, and throw them all to the Burners if that's what it takes. And nothing you do is going to stop me."

He steps forward and grabs my face in his hands. His touch is rough, but I do not budge. "I won't forget you. You've helped me learn some invaluable lessons along the way. I wouldn't be able to do any of this had it not been for you."

"You're a sociopath," I say.

"And you're a hypocrite," he snaps. He pushes my face away and wrings his hands. "You were all too willing to haunt your friends when it suited your stupid high school vendetta. But when it's my turn to do something bigger, something extraordinary, I'm the bad guy? No. No one is innocent here. It's a brave new world, Sarah. And since you're not on board, you're just in my way. Good-bye. Sweet dreams." He smiles. "I'm sure you'll be seeing me."

With that, he turns and walks away.

I watch him disappear, my heart thumping. I didn't create this monster, but I helped him grow. And Wes is right; we can do things no one else can, and we understand each other like no one else does.

Which is why I am the only one who can take him down.

I dive into the crowd, weaving through bodies until I find Grady and Tessa. Grabbing them both by the hands, I ignore their confused protests as I drag them off the field and away from the light into what promises to be a very long night.

chapter twenty-three

I look at the two people I've just confessed the whole, unabridged truth to. Tessa and Grady sit cross-legged on Grady's bed, slack-jawed. It's a lot to digest, I know. I've been living with my ability to enter people's dreams and possess their bodies, and I still have trouble believing it. But keeping this from Tessa is no longer an option. I need her. And Grady? Well, he's my Hail Mary. He already knows something's up, so why not tap his massive brain to help me figure out the rest?

Pursing his lips, Grady runs his hand through his pumpkin-colored hair and says, "I knew it."

Tessa's eyes bug. "You knew it? Knew what, exactly? That Sarah thinks she's hanging out in our heads while we sleep, or that she's dating Freddie Krueger?"

Grady blushes. "Well, no, I didn't know the details, but I knew something was going on, and now it all makes sense."

She snorts. "Oh yeah, total sense."

Though I know it's unfair of me, I can't help but feel a little crushed that Tessa thinks I'm nuts. Still, there's no time for hurt feelings. I remind myself that Grady's openness is what's important. His mind is what I need.

"So how do I stop Wes?" I ask eagerly.

"Good question," he says. "I don't know. But I'm guessing the answer lies within your disorder. So let's break it down. Seems to me that what you're experiencing is part chemistry, part mythology. The chemistry is actually pretty simple. Dexidnipam is made up of two main components: a controlled-release hypnotic and an anticonvulsant, correct?"

"Yeah, it puts me to sleep, and it keeps me from moving."

"That's what I said," he replies dryly. "The thing is, these homeostatic functions are a focus of our nervous system while we sleep. Maintaining them is its primary job. And the fact that your body isn't doing them means that the things it actually does do while you're asleep are intensified. Like how a blind person has a better-than-normal sense of smell. Since your body isn't using energy to keep you still, it can pour that energy into the other things your body does while you sleep—so your dream state is heightened. Make sense?"

"Yeah," I say. "I think so."

He goes on. "I'm guessing that when you're given enough

hypnotic to actually stay asleep and enough paralytic to keep you from moving, your body proportionately increases your anabolic functions to compensate. Your EEG readings are off the charts, right?"

"That's what they say at the clinic," I reply. "I have a very active frontal lobe."

"Of course," he says, clapping his hands as his pitch rises. "The part of the brain that controls lucid dreaming!"

Tessa raises a hand to halt the celebration. "Hold up. Rewind. What are you two talking about? What other things Sarah does while she's asleep? We don't *do* anything while we're asleep. That's why it's called *sleeping*."

Grady shakes his head. "And I'm the one who gets picked on."

"Tess, I know it seems crazy," I say.

"Try impossible," she shoots back.

"Impossible," I agree patiently. "But it's not. I have never lied to you, and I'm not starting now. Even if you can't believe me, could you please just go with it for the sake of this conversation? For me?"

She stares at me hard, a mixture of concern, confusion, and suspicion contorting her face, but she doesn't protest.

I turn my attention back to Grady. "So what is my frontal lobe so much better at than regular people's?"

"Well," he says. "There are things we know about. Like, when you sleep, your brain cells shrink so that waste matter can easily move through your brain and get flushed out of your system. There's a fascinating study linking this waste management process to the reduction of the protein involved in Alzheimer's. It's a great read."

"Awesome," Tessa chirps. "Sarah won't forget who I am when she's a hundred!" She glares at Grady. "If I have to go with this, you need to stay on topic. So tell us, genius. What does any of this have to do with Sarah voodoo-dolling Gigi?"

Grady pushes his glasses up on the bridge of his nose purposefully. "Well, delta wave and REM sleep are still pretty mysterious. There are a multitude of functions that we don't remotely understand, and sleep science is a relatively new field of study. So while we can look at a brain scan and see that all these areas, which are dormant while we're awake, light up when we're asleep, that doesn't mean we have a clue what these parts of the brain are actually doing during that time."

He pauses and takes a deep breath for effect. "That's where mythology comes in."

"Mythology?" I ask.

"Mythology," he repeats. "Just about every culture has a favorite story or theory that explains why our bodies shut down for the night and what the visions that occur during that time mean. The Greeks had Morpheus, who delivered prophetic messages from the gods through dreams. The Ojibwe dreamcatcher was hung to trap nightmares that disrupted the restorative sleep time. And in more recent philosophical belief, Jung suggested that there's a collective unconscious, shared by all people, that we can access in dreams."

"The train station," I say. "Where Wes and I find people on Dexid."

"No," Grady replies dispassionately. "But also, maybe yes. Jung was talking about an inherited unconscious way of ordering and understanding the world that each individual utilizes to process his or her own personal experience."

"English!" Tessa yells.

Grady sighs. "In dreams, we all have the same basic ways of trying to work out the personal problems that we can't solve while we're awake. Reductive enough for you?"

She fake-smiles.

"But you make me wonder," he adds ominously. "What if that shared space was in fact tangible? After you fall asleep, when you wake up in unconsciousness, you said you're in a train station?"

"Yeah, Grand Central," I say.

"Why Grand Central?" Tessa asks.

"Yeah, why Grand Central?" Grady echoes.

They look at me expectantly, but I have no answer. I've never before wondered why I've entered the train station every night since I've been on the Dexid, what the significance of the space or location is. But when I open my mouth to say as much, a forgotten truth comes out instead.

"Ralphie, my tech, mentioned it to me my first night in the clinic. I was asking him what to expect while on the Dexid, and he told me another patient visualized the train station once they fell asleep."

Grady claps his hands together, causing Tessa to squeak. "That's great! That explains it."

"Yeah, I totally get it now," she sasses.

"The train station is just a construct," Grady says, ignoring her. "An imagined space you've clung to so that you could order the void. I'm guessing Wes was either the patient who first imagined Grand Central or the tech planted the same visual with him right before he fell asleep for the first time on Dexid. Either way, it was just breadcrumbs to lead you to where you needed to be: an actualized shared unconsciousness into which you, Sarah, can astral project. You and Wes are like shamans, metaphysically traveling into a nonphysical realm where the rules of our reality do not apply."

I stare at Grady, speechless. Part of me wants to shout for joy, to thank him for not just believing but understanding my impossible reality, while the other part of me is so overwhelmed by the possible truth of it that I feel like I'm about to cry. Before I can put any of this into words, Tessa chimes in.

"Okay, wait," she says slowly. "Not that I'm on board with any of this, but for the sake of argument, I think I get the shaman thing. Don't they believe that, like, the mind isn't in the body to begin with? And if you drink some nasty concoction, you can get into other people and sort of control them?"

Grady and I stare at her, impressed.

"What?" she says with a shrug. "I know things too." Dexterously, she grabs a brownie bite from the bag I bought at the bake sale and tosses it into her mouth.

"Today's most potent concoctions come in pill form," Grady says. "The Dexid must have allowed you to connect with other people who had been narcotically induced into this state of literalized collective unconscious."

"Like you were," I say.

"Like I was," he agrees. "But when I took the Dexid, I became a passive participant in that realm. Unlike you who, thanks to those mysterious functions that grow exponentially when you take that drug, is able to be in total, active control. And the more you took, the more control you had. Not just of yourself but of the entire Dexid-shared unconscious space and anyone in it."

"But not just me," I say.

"No," he replies solemnly. "Not just you."

The specter of Wes has entered the room and brought us back to terrifying reality.

"Why me and Wes?" I ask. "There are other people in the Dexid trial, but they're not jumping into anyone else's skin."

"Anyone else with RBD?" Tessa asks. "Any other kids?"

I shake my head.

Grady taps the side of his glasses. "Maybe it's your disorder. Maybe it's your brain. You know the brain is still very much under construction in adolescence, developing key parts of the cortex and contending with more gray matter than scientists once thought. Add to that the incredibly volatile and unpredictable hormonal changes of the teen years, and it's no wonder you and Wes have a unique response to an untested drug. But whatever the reason, the fact remains, you are special. And so is Wes."

For a while, we're all quiet, not knowing what else to say. Tessa shoves more brownie into her mouth in a helpless let-them-eat-cake sort of way. I join her.

Finally, she breaks the silence. "Oh, I know. Why don't we just keep the Dexid away from Wes? I mean, without it, he's just a creep. So if we make sure that Wes can't dose anyone or take a pill himself, we're in the clear, right?"

Grady smiles. "That's brilliant. All things being equal, the simplest answer is the right one. Occam's razor."

"Uh, sure," Tessa says.

"I took the Dexid myself," Grady offers. "But how did you guys dose Gigi and the rest without them knowing? I assume you used the stash I gave you?"

"Yeah," I say, feeling the absolute definition of ashamed. "But Wes was in charge of the dosing. And to tell the truth, I never knew how he did it."

"Well, he definitely didn't hand them a pill," Tessa says. She begins to yawn, speaking before she's finished. "There's no way any one of them would take drugs from a stranger. Except maybe Amber."

Grady nods. "Gigi and Kiara never did anything harder than alcohol. Maybe the occasional joint. Generally, jock girls don't do much for my business."

"Poor you," Tessa says as she stretches. She leans in for the last brownie bite, but Grady snatches it in protest and shoves it in his mouth.

"Regardless," I say, "we used up all the pills you gave us, and the clinic only doles out a week's worth at a time. So, Wes probably has only two or three left after he dosed Jamie and took his own pills last night. On the downside, that's one full night of damage. On the upside, it's only one night."

A pained grunt escapes Grady's lips as all the redness drains from his face.

"What?" I ask.

"In my defense," he says, "I had no idea about any of this at the time. I just assumed he wanted to rough up Josh for letting Gigi take the photos of you."

"Who wanted to... Wes wanted to beat up Josh? Grady, what are you talking about?"

Tessa yawns loudly. "Sorry, sorry," she says as she lazily rubs her head. Her eyes start to glaze over. "I'm just going to lay down for a minute."

My spidey-sense begins to tingle as she leans back on Grady's bed.

"Yesterday, Wes asked me to set up a meeting with Josh," he says. "He gave me some cash and made me promise never to bring it up. As I said, I thought he wanted to kick that loser's ass, which was fine with me. Josh is a douche. I had no idea Wes was after more Dexid."

I register this very bad news, but when I try to gasp, a yawn comes out instead. I look over at Tessa, who is cuddling up with a pillow.

"Gigi would never take a pill from Wes," I say. "But if it was hidden in something else…"

The only thing Wes learned from boarding school was how to slip a girl a roofie undetected, I think. My stomach drops to the center of the earth, and I trip on my feet as I scramble over the bed to Tessa.

I shake her hard. "How many brownies did you eat?"

"Huh?" she asks groggily.

"How many brownie bites did you eat? The ones from the bake sale. The ones I bought?"

For a brief moment, she's wide awake. "Five, six? I ate six of them."

"Genius," Grady mutters. I glare at him. "I mean, uh-oh. Be right back." He runs to the bathroom and makes himself puke up the Dexid-laced baked good.

"Listen to me, Tessa," I say desperately. "Wes won't hurt you if I'm there. He just wants me. And I'll be with you soon. You'll be okay. I promise."

I try not to let her see the panic that screams inside me. Tessa will be asleep and vulnerable to Wes within moments. How much did I eat? How soon will I be in the dream with her? With him?

"I should have known he was after you that first time we saw him," Tessa says, the fear subtle but evident in her exhausted voice.

"Wes?"

She yawns again, and I follow suit. "He was too quick to smack down Gigi for a girl he'd never even met before."

"You mean in the hallway at school?" I shake my head, which is starting to feel awfully heavy. "No, remember? I told you tonight. That wasn't the first time he and I saw each other. It was a few nights before, the night of the sleepover. Wes was in my dream in the woods."

I still. How could I not have realized this sooner? The first time I ever saw Wes, the first dream I shared with him, took place in the preserve behind the Horsemen's football field. It didn't originate in the train station, because it was my dream.

"And I wasn't on Dexid," I say out loud.

Grady's right. Everyone has access to the dream realm, whether they're on Dexid or not. We each make sense of it in our own way. Wes's train station is just another version of my nature preserve, of Grady's carnival, of Gigi's kitchen. We order the chaos of the unknown to control it.

Only Wes and I are different from everyone else. Since we were kids, our bodies have reacted to our dreams in a way that other peoples' don't. That gave us access to the entirety of the dream world; we just didn't know it until the magic cocktail of RBD, teenaged hormones, and Dexid brought our conscious thought into the game. It's how I found Tessa in her dream at the beach and how Wes found me in the woods. The doorway into each other's dreams has always been there—the Dexid just gives us the key to unlock it.

Now I have to slam the door shut.

"Tessa, when you fall asleep, go to the woods behind the school. Hide in the trees and wait for me. I'll find you there."

"The woods," she repeats on an exhale.

"I'll be there soon," I say. My limbs start to tingle. "I won't let him hurt you."

She looks at me through half-closed lids before falling deeply asleep.

Grady appears in the doorway to his room.

My eyes are heavy now. "He'll be on more Dexid, so he'll be stronger than me," I say, my words beginning to slur.

"Then be smarter than him," Grady replies. "You just told Tessa that you weren't even on Dexid the first time you saw Wes, right? Use that. You may need the Dexid to control other people, but not to take on Wes. You two *are* special. You really are linked. But while he's whining about it, you can use it. Use everything you know that he doesn't to gain an advantage. Give me the list."

"I don't need the Dexid to reach him," I mumble as I lie down beside Tessa.

Grady nods.

"The train station isn't real."

He kneels beside me. "Because there is no physical landscape. Ignore the architecture. It's all just there to order something you don't understand. So stop relying on it. Break through it. Wes believes he's living outside the box. But you know there isn't any box at all."

The length of my blinking is getting longer now. Another yawn forces its way out.

"I've seen you on the field, Sarah," Grady says, his voice

distant, as if coming from the far end of a tunnel. "You're a killer. So take him out."

My eyelids slide shut.

I am asleep.

chapter twenty-four

....

*B*link—*darkness*
　　Blink—fog
Blink—light, dim and distant
Blink—growing brighter now
Blink—shining, hot
Blink—like a spotlight
Blink—like staring into the sun
Blink—like going blind
Blink—it's blinding me
Blink—it's BLINDING me
Blink—it's—
<gasp>
I suck in air like I'm breaking the surface of water that I've been submerged in for almost too long. Shielding my eyes from a train's glaring

headlight, I stumble over metal tracks until I find a wall against which to steady myself.

I take a moment to acclimate to my surroundings. I'm in the tunnels of Grand Central, directly in the path of an idling train…that's not real. If I concentrate hard enough, I don't have to see it. Don't think outside the box. Know there is no box. I focus on my breathing, let my vision blur. I feel no tension, no stress, nothing closing in on or confining me.

The train vanishes.

The walls fall away.

I'm standing in the thick, gray fog of my very first dream with Wes, before the Dexid, the night I tried to kill Gigi. And there is nothing but the misty void that once bored me. What I'd give for such a banal complaint now.

I push my way through nothingness until I notice a glow ahead on my right. A door. Luminous, gleaming softly. There's another one across, on my left, and yet another beyond that. A corridor of dreams just waiting for me to enter. All the people Wes dosed. How many are there? Where is he? And where is Tessa?

Tessa. Tie her up, I think. Why didn't I tell Grady to tie her up? I was too tired, too focused on Wes. But if I had told him to do that one thing, Tessa would be safe. I look at the glowing doors around me. But that wouldn't have helped the other dreamers. What is Wes planning to do to them?

I travel on, stopping at a door. Faded mahogany, slightly ajar. My hand reaches out to push the handle, but I stop short as the air heats up, the fog grows denser. A smell of what—rot?—curls my nostrils, and a low grumble drums in my ears.

Primal fear saps my concentration, and the architecture of the train station—Wes's train station—reconstructs itself around me. I am inside the car but outside a dream, looking directly into the mangled face of a hungry Burner.

I stumble backward, unintentionally pinning myself against the glass partition of the sliding door's vestibule. The Burner looks directly at me, right into my very soul, and snarls. It's over. There's nowhere to go, no way to hide. I'm in arm's reach of the one thing that can prevent me from stopping Wes before I've had the chance to try. I brace myself for impact.

But the Burner doesn't take me.

It grunts through its nose, like a horse on a cold morning. Then it retreats to stand sentinel in the doorway of the dream.

I am safe.

But why?

Why didn't it devour me, stop me before I could get anywhere near the dreamer? I stand in the open car and watch as the Burner patrols the inside of this dream. It registers my presence every time it passes by the door, but it never makes a move toward me. It's playing defense by holding the line. It's waiting for something else to come—protecting the dreamer from something that's much bigger and badder than I am.

"Oh, Wes," I whisper to myself. "How much Dexid did you take?"

I look around the train and am shocked by what I see. The cabin is empty. Not a single commuter. Paper and garbage litter the compartment, and graffiti defaces the walls. This is not the gleaming car I know. This place is poisoned. I run ahead.

I pass sliding doors in various states of access. Some are closed; most are either partially or fully open. They all reveal different dreamscapes on the other side. All featuring my classmates.

In one doorway, Trisha Goldmark runs from a blood-soaked madman through a frozen forest, while my sixth grade crush, Denny Kringle, treads croc-infested swamp water in another. Across from him, Christa from the bake sale weeps as a half pig, half woman hybrid shoves forkful after forkful of chocolate cake into her mouth. Tears and chocolate smear her face as a Burner appears in the doorway of her nightmare.

Because that's what these are—nightmares. Nightmares because the Burners are inside them, their general being of disease infecting the subconscious of the dreamer. Another thing to thank me and Wes for.

Wes. Where is he?

I soften my eyes, empty my mind, see past the architecture of the train. There is a subtle glow nearby, like in Jamie's dream, dancing in my peripheral vision. I turn toward it, hoping it will lead me to Wes, hoping it can help me understand why he's doing this.

Before I can take a step, an object manifests in the ethereal fog, defines itself as...an arm. It clotheslines me. I crumple to the ground with an audible, "Oof." The walls of the train snap back into place, imprisoning me as Wes comes into focus. He kneels beside me as I catch my breath.

"You came," he says brightly.

"Did I have a choice?" I ask through grinding teeth. As I pull myself to a seated position, I scoot closer to Christa's dream, Burner and all. I want as much distance between me and the real monster as possible. "How many people did you dose, Wes?"

He shrugs. "Not sure. I let the bake sale gods decide. Well, mostly," he adds, playful, flirtatious. *"I did make sure a couple of special guests were invited."* The impish smirk beams, and my fury rises. *"How many did you eat before you realized?"*

I do not reply.

That once-sexy, now-infuriating grin widens. "Come on, Sarah. Admit it. You're glad to be here. You wanted to come. You can't stop wanting to be here. To be with me. To—"

"I'm not here for you," I snap, his interminable refrain getting the better of me. *Though I stop myself before I say her name, I can see the realization the moment it hits him. I am such an idiot.*

"Tessa!" he cries with delight. *"Tessa's here."*

"No," I lie.

Wes chuckles as he turns and scans the doors. "I wonder which one is hers."

The now-familiar feeling of panic sets in. "Wes. Do not touch her."

He ignores me. "It's kind of poetic, don't you think? I mean, technically, you were the one who gave her the laced brownies, not me. You're the one responsible for her being here at all." He faces me. "But if you'd like, we can make a deal."

I tense. "What kind of deal?"

"I'll trade you all these poor, defenseless dreamers—promise not to harm a hair on any one of their sweet, innocent heads—if you give up Tessa." His eyes narrow, and the smile vanishes. "I'll walk her down the middle of a dark highway at four a.m. or guzzle pint after pint of castor oil until she bursts all the blood vessels in her eyeballs puking it up. I'll beat the crap out of her sleeping body, anything I want, and you won't do a thing about it. Except watch."

"Bite me," I snap, my saliva curdling.

"Been there, done that," he snarls back. He looks down at me, lust now turned to disgust. "It's time I move on. What we had was fun, but you have an embarrassing lack of imagination. I've got big dreams, and you're focused on petty problems. What's that Emerson quote? A foolish consistency is the hobgoblin of little minds."

"Right," I scoff. "Because I don't want to hurt people just for the fun of it. I know Mommy and Stepdad didn't love you enough, but isn't anarchistic destruction a bit of a clichéd way to act out?"

"God, you're boring." He turns and walks down the aisle.

I jump to my feet and hurry after him. If nothing else, I can try to slow him down, because the longer I keep his attention on me, the less time he has to find Tessa.

"What if this isn't you, Wes? What if it's the Dexid making you act like this? I remember how weird I felt when we took four pills. I wasn't in my right mind. It affected my judgement. I thought of doing things I'd never—"

"Ugh, this again?" He stops short, and it's all I can do not to slam into him. "That was your thing, not mine. It isn't my problem if you can't handle your drugs. I'm fine. In fact, I'm great." He shakes his head. "You know, Sarah, I liked you for you. Why can't you get that I'm really still me but, like, a thousand times better. I feel fantastic, and there's nothing wrong with that." He peers through a doorway into a dream.

No Tessa.

It's like we're playing Russian roulette, and though I've survived one more round, the bullet creeps closer.

"That's what addicts say," I remark.

Wes continues down the aisle. "You know, that's total bull, right? It's true, I don't care about any of these people. They're dull and weak. But neither did you when we were enacting your little revenge plays."

"I seem to recall that was originally your idea," I say.

He peers into another sliding door, and I hold my breath until I see a bookworm sophomore racing through library stacks as heavy tomes spill down on her.

"But it was your desire," he replies. "They embarrassed you, so you embarrassed them. An eye for an eye." He looks at me hard. "And you loved it."

My face flushes. I hate it, but Wes is right. I can tell myself that I was blinded by lust, but who am I kidding? It wasn't just Wes I was in love with. It was control. It was power.

He reaches another door before I realize I've stopped moving. As I run to catch up with him, he starts back. A Burner growls at him from across the threshold of the doorway but doesn't cross it. He laughs.

"You see this?" he says. "Just like I said at the vigil, the Burners got smart. They learned from their little two-step with Jamie. They don't want to enter the dreamer, on purpose or by accident. But they need to stop us from doing it. So now they're staying close to their wards instead of going out looking for us. Which is absolutely fantastic!"

He approaches the doorway, and the Burner faces him on the other side. Wes is right. It doesn't make a move to catch him. "See? This is how to manage them. Take enough Dexid and dose enough dreamers so the beasts stand guard inside their dreams."

"You mean one Burner is assigned to each dream?" I ask, fascinated in spite of myself. "And they stay there? No matter what?"

He nods and points to the metal saddle on the floor that creates a border between train car and dream. "They won't chase me unless I cross that threshold. All I have to do is wait for Ugly to patrol past the door, slip into the dream, and make it to the dreamer first. Not so hard when its one-on-one. Because if I go into just one dream at a time, there's only one Burner to contend with—no one's coming as backup. I get the monster to fall into the dreamer, and poof! I can take each Burner out one by one." He smiles in the beast's face, taunting him. "I love this!"

I look at the snarling monster. It wants a piece of Wes so bad, it can barely contain itself. If only I could get it out of the dream, out here—get all of them out here at once. But how?

Wes struts to the next dream door. "For once, I'm not the lab rat. They are. And I'm conducting the experiment. This is my calling. My life's work. To understand this vast mysterious landscape as I become king of it. To bring order and control to the chaos. To discover—"

"Hey, Wes," I interrupt. "Do you know what the best part is of having dumped your sorry ass? I don't have to listen to your stupid bullshit." I lurch toward the nearest dream and throw my arm across the threshold of the open sliding door. The Burner that's been on patrol is suddenly free, and I swear I see its mangled, monstrous face smile.

The beast comes crashing through the doorway, out of the dream, tumbling awkwardly onto the train car floor. Wes looks back, stilled by confusion until fear lights a fire under his ass. The Burner gets to its feet and roars.

Wes runs. So do I.

I run after him through the train, throwing my hand, foot, elbow, whatever body part is closest into every dream doorway I pass, releasing

Burner after Burner after Burner. Wes is too busy saving himself to realize what I'm doing at first. And we make it through another car and a half before it dawns on him. Suddenly, he stops, turns, and tackles me. We fly through an open dream doorway and fall into...

A classroom.

Undecorated.

Sterile.

Fluorescent lights cast a slightly jaundiced glow over the scene. At every desk is a student taking a test. Army personnel patrol the aisles, daring cheaters to make their day. And on the board are three letters: S.A.T.

The dream seems innocuous enough, not like the nightmares I've encountered elsewhere on the train. Then I see Meat Butchowski, Grady's older brother, sitting at a desk center stage, directly under the brightest fluorescent in the room. He hasn't made a single mark on his test, and he's sweating from every pore on his body. And I literally mean every one of them, because I can see them all. Meat is taking the SATs, utterly clueless and completely naked.

I flush, embarrassed for both the dreamer and myself, but I get over it the second I catch something moving in my periphery. Wes runs from the opposite side of the classroom, right for Meat. I push past a soldier and slide across a desk. I reach Meat a second before Wes, but that's all I need to jump into his body first.

Whoosh.
Pop.

The lights are on in Meat's room. He's fallen asleep at his desk. I rub the sleep out of his eyes and push back on his rolling chair. I throw the door to his bedroom open and run across the hall.

"Hey, door's closed for a reason," Grady says as I—Meat—push our way into his room.

"Secure Tessa," I order in a register at least two octaves below my own.

"Sarah?" Grady asks as he looks from Meat to my body lying motionless beside Tessa on his bed. He's white as sugar. "Of course, I-I'll protect her," he stutters.

I shake Meat's head. "No, I mean secure her literally. Tie her up."

He stares at me.

"Grady, can you do that?" I demand. "Answer me."

"Yes. Yes, I can do that."

"Good. Now hit me—Meat—and tie him up too."

"What?" He looks at me in horror.

"It's the only way for me to exit his body," I say, "and you can't tell me you've never wanted to punch your brother."

"Well, yeah, but...Sarah, wait. There's something else."

"What?" I snap. I have to get back to the station.

"After you left, I was thinking."

"No time for thinking, Grady. Hit me!"

He ignores me but speeds up. "Just because you and Wes are different in the same way doesn't mean you're alike. The Dexid might have opened you up to your shared abilities, but it doesn't dictate what you do with them."

"Meaning what?"

"Just because you're both high doesn't mean you're on the same trip."

"Too many metaphors," I warn. "I need battle tactics."

"Wes is an addict," he blurts. "Give him an overdose."

Pop.

Grady's words are lost in the space between Meat's body and his dream. I am lying on the ground beside the dreamer, but I don't remember Grady hitting me. Then I realize he hasn't.

Wes is inside Meat now. He jumped in and booted me out, just like I did to him the night we haunted Gigi.

I watch a possessed, naked Meat run around the nightmare classroom, knocking over desks, steamrolling through soldiers, and barreling into students. I cringe at what damage the six foot two linebacker is doing in the waking world, when he suddenly stops and collapses to the ground. Wes falls out, and I smile.

Grady totally just nailed his brother.

The half dozen Burners I released from the other dreams pour in through the doorway, and there's no time to waste. I am on my feet and running. I concentrate, blur my eyes, search through the fog, and notice an area ahead with a slight glow to it. It has to be the dream's exit. Pretty soon, Wes is beside me. He's no fool. He might not know how I've figured it out, but he knows where I'm headed. I throw open the door to a janitor's closet, and we exit the dream.

We're back in the dirty train car, and the Burners are not far behind. Wes takes off down the aisle, glancing in every dream door that he passes. He's about four doors down when something catches his eye, and he stops. He looks back at me and smiles. It's a playful, dangerous grin that chills me to my soul. Please, God, don't be Tessa.

He jumps into the dream.

I follow.

Unlike Meat's fluorescent dream, this one is midnight blue, dark, and shadowy. It takes me a minute to adjust my eyes, blinking a surreal landscape into focus. It's the clinic, my clinic, the place where this all began. I follow dim lights, blinking on and off in a chaotic rhythm, down a corridor of patient and observation rooms. Zombified people groan in their beds while faceless techs listlessly go about their mindless tasks: taking vitals, reading printouts, entering data. Over and over again.

A howl echoes down the hallway, and I keep moving, aware that the Burners are close behind. I search every room I pass, wondering whose dream I'm in and where I will find Wes, when a catcall whistle guides my search. I follow the sound to an observation room, where I see Wes standing just a few feet away from the dreamer: Josh Mowrey.

"The Burners will be here any second," he says. "But if we set up Josh like a bowling pin and slip out of the way as they strike, he'll get what's coming to him, and we can get out." He smiles blithely, and my hands ball into fists. "So are you with me?" he asks. "Or will you be noble and go down for this perverted jackass?"

It's the perfect dilemma. I can save myself by being the utter hypocrite Wes says I am—that he wants me to be—or be ejected from the dream realm and wake up in Burner-induced paralysis with no way to help Tessa.

"Had it not been for Gigi, this predator would've done way worse to you," he slyly reminds me. "You know how good payback feels. And let's be honest. The Pollyanna look just isn't you." The taunting snark suddenly disappears, and quietly, thoughtfully, he adds, "Make the honest choice, Sarah. Even if it's not the right one."

I glance at the door, which rattles from the weight of heavy, advancing footsteps. That way will lead me into the arms of the Burners, with no hope of protecting Tessa or bringing Wes down. But even if I refuse to hurt Josh, Wes will jump into his body or throw him to the Burners and make his escape.

I look at Josh. He's done for, no matter what. And the sick truth is, I really don't care. Wes is right. If I'm completely honest, I feel a little pleasure in knowing he'll finally be punished for his sins.

But this decision isn't about Josh. It's about me. I nod my head as I accept the fact that the bad choices and dark deeds were not all Wes's doing. They were mine too. And it's high time I stop them from happening again.

"Fine," I say, heading for Josh as the Burners burst into the room. Wes's eyes twinkle as he relishes my fall. The only thing better than confronting me with my true nature is having manipulated me into doing so myself. But as Grady said, there are some things Wes doesn't know. The twinkle disappears as the Burners rush toward us. I pivot before I reach Josh and throw my body into Wes's.

I relax my eyes
my breath
my mind
and break free of the dream

break free of the box

because I know there isn't any box at all.

We fall backward, through the floor, and into the fog, where there are no walls and no rules.

My stomach drops like on the first dip of a roller coaster. For a moment, we are flying through the void, and I savor it. There's a freedom to this release. I might have fallen all night in this nothingness had I been alone. But I'm not. As Wes digs his teeth into my shoulder, I lose my focus, and we slam into the ground.

We're back on the train, inside the box Wes has constructed. Immediately, he's on me, and we grapple on the floor. Wes grabs my arm and twists it behind my back. I yell as I thrust the pinky finger of my free hand deep into his ear canal. He howls in pain. His fingers wrap around chunks of hair on either side of my head, and I scream as he lifts me from my roots. I'm kicking, biting at air, but when he smashes my skull down hard against the train floor, the fight stops. My peripheral vision completely blacks out, and all I can see is his body drag itself away from me. Slow at first, he picks up speed as he runs down the long, narrow aisle of my tunnel vision and into the next car of the train.

There's a low rumble. The Burners have picked up our scent. I stumble to my feet and shake my head to excise the ringing that goes from ear to ear. My vision fights its way back as I move awkwardly down the aisle, steadying myself with a tight grip as I move from seat to seat until I can limp after Wes on my own. Groaning, grunting, and growling chokes the air behind me, but I don't look back.

Ahead of me, I see a bright glowing orb beside a set of sliding dream doors. Try as he might, Wes can't shake me. I will always find him. He's disappeared into a dream, but before long, I'm there too. Exhausted and bruised but determined, I tumble, head first, into...

Leaves.

Brittle.

Crunching.

Thick.

They engulf me. They're sticking to my clothes, tangled in my hair. I raise myself on elbows, and as I brush them away, I realize where I am. The nature preserve behind the Horsemen's football field. Where I told Tessa to go before she fell asleep.

I'm in her dream.

I pull myself to my feet and begin searching for her, knowing that somewhere in this dream, Wes is too.

I stumble over rocks and roots and pebbly paths. I become clumsy as my desperation deepens, and I fall, scraping my hands and knees. I know what's coming, and I'm terrified.

Snarls and moans mingle with the whistling windy air. The Burners are closing in, and I've no way of knowing how close they are or how many have come. But it doesn't matter, so long as I get to Tessa and Wes first.

Then...

The trees thin as they open onto a clearing.

Tessa sits quietly at its center.

Wes stands beside her.

I start to speak, but it's pointless.

He jumps

into

> *her*

>> *body.*

I race over to Tessa and watch, helpless, as she falls backward to the ground. Her eyes glaze over as her body begins to twitch, then shudder, then jerk. She looks like she's having one hell of an epileptic fit, but she doesn't get up. She remains on her back, writhing but not moving more than a foot in any direction.

I exhale relief. Tessa is safe. Grady tied her up, just like I asked him to. Wes can't do anything to her body; he can't even knock himself out to return to the dreams. He's trapped.

I take a moment to breathe. To steel myself against the awful decision I've made. The only choice I have left.

I sit beside my best friend's quivering body until, finally, she stills. Can Wes guess what's coming? Is he making a plan? Or has he accepted his fate?

The grunts and growls grow louder as the Burners circle the clearing. I cannot tell how many there are. Drawn by the massive amount of Dexid in Wes's system, they look infinite. They are everywhere, surrounding us.

As they come toward me in an enormous heaving mass, I lean down beside Tessa and whisper in her ear.

"I'm so sorry, Wes," I say. "I wish it didn't have to end like this."

Then I jump into Tessa's body and push Wes out.

My eyes open on a flushed face. Grady holds a heavy book above my head. "Hit me," I command. "Now."

His Adam's apple bulges as he swallows his fear and brings the encyclopedia down.

An agonized scream fills my ears as I return to my best friend's nightmare, and it takes me a moment to realize that the cry is not my own. I look over to see Wes tangled up in a thicket of Burners, struggling as they crush him tighter and tighter.

Overdose, *I think.*

His wild eyes meet mine for just a second. Then I too am enveloped in a Burner's cold embrace, and we both dissolve into the dark nothingness of the hungry, paralyzing beasts.

chapter twenty-five

Whoosh.

The automatic doors open to the overpowering perfume of antiseptic cleaner. There's a secondary smell that I hadn't been able to place the first few weeks I was coming here, but now, after a month and a half of daily visits, I recognize the odor lurking behind every Clorox-wiped surface for what it is: sick. I suppose that's what you get in a hospital. Whether the patients recover or relapse, one way or another, they move on. But the imprint of illness they leave behind never disappears, no matter how hard the janitors scrub.

I wave to Hugo, the weekday security guard who has my visitor's badge waiting. "Think today could be the day, Miss Reyes," he says as he hands me the adhesive nametag.

"Fingers crossed," I chirp, and Hugo gives me a thumbs-up.

He started making this statement after my sixth consecutive visit, and now it's become a thing. I doubt either one of us considers the meaning of the words anymore. It's more about ritual than hope. But the ritual is just as important to me now. Routine is what keeps me going.

I take my badge and proceed on my daily route: main hallway, first left, second right, elevators up to the fifth floor.

The doors open on a nurse's station. A nurse named Donna looks up sternly from her charts, but her face softens into a forlorn friendliness when she sees it's me. She waves me through. I give her a polite smile, turn left, and follow a long hallway to room 529.

Donna's type of pity is something I've become very familiar with in the past few months. First, when Gigi threw me out of the cool clique at school. Next, in the aftermath of Jamie's accident. Then, on the faces of the FDA agents who interviewed me about the horrible side effects of the drug Dexidnipam. And now, as the devoted girlfriend of the boy in the coma in room 529.

The coma.

When I "woke up" from my Burner-induced paralysis after Wes and I were expelled from Tessa's dream, I was in the hospital, surrounded by doctors who all had endless questions about my harrowing experience on Dexidnipam. I'd seen no need to mention the dream sharing or body snatching, because, between my testimony about the nightmares and temporary paralysis it induced and the fact that another patient in the trial was now in a coma, Dexid's shelf life had been indefinitely shelved. But for a good couple of weeks, I was hounded with specific questions I pretended I couldn't answer. Like why Wes had exponentially more Dexid in his system than I did.

Sure, I could have tried to explain it all, but Wes had been right about at least one thing. All that the truth would have elicited was a trip to the loony bin for me and more experiments on him. No matter how things had gone down between us, I could never allow that.

Especially when I knew he was really awake.

It had been Grady's words about addiction and overdose that guided my actions that night. The only real way to take Wes out and save my classmates had been to overload his system, not with more Dexid, but with as many Burners as we could attract. I can only guess that Wes had taken so much of the drug that when the monsters attacked him, they not only expelled him from the dream realm, but also caused an immobility and unresponsiveness in the waking world that was so complete, the doctors classified him as comatose. Only one monster came for me—the higher amount of Dexid in Wes's system attracting the vast majority of the beasts— and I lay locked in my body for only a few hours. The untold number of Burners that infected Wes froze him in a waking paralysis that's been going strong for twenty-three days and counting.

I push open the door to room 529 and take a deep breath. Just as he had the day before and the week before that, Wes lies unmoving on a hospital cot, his hands and head hooked up to machines that tell his doctors absolutely nothing about what's really going on inside him. I let the door click closed as I walk to his bed and hoist myself onto the mattress beside him. Leaning over his chest, I place my fingers on his eyelids and push them open.

"Hey," I say and conjure a smile. "It's a beautiful Friday. Sixty-eight degrees outside and kind of sunny. Not a bad day to wake up." I look at his fingers, knowing from personal experience that when you're trapped like this, the extremities are always the first to regain movement. But there's not a twitch.

"Not ready to move yet? Okay, then how about some gossip? Gigi 2.0 continues her reign, albeit a slightly less bitchy one. That healthy dose of paranoia that our sleep stalking gave her might actually have paid off, just like you said it would. Jackie Dahl spilled a particularly vomitus container of tapioca pudding on Ms. MacDonald's new leather jacket this morning, and for a second, it totally looked like Gigi was going to hurl her fist into Jackie's face. But then she smiled and kind of laughed it off. Progress, right?"

I glance at Wes's mouth, waiting for it to curl into that twisty grin. But his lips remain taught in a straight line, slightly parted and a little chapped. I make a mental note to bring lip balm tomorrow.

"What else? Um…Amber seems to be less and less okay with standing just outside of Gigi's spotlight. Even though with Kiara gone, she's top minion again, she's been seen out and about without Gigi, and I swear she's back-talked her master in public more than a few times. I foresee a falling out before graduation. Might want to wake up for that. Could be entertaining."

I pause, but the beeping machines are the closest thing I get to a laugh track.

"And Jamie's rehab is going really well. They told him yesterday that there's almost no chance he'll ever play football again, which made him even more determined to walk by Christmas." I chuckle. "If anyone can do it—" I stop myself, because now I'm just being mean.

No matter how pissed I am at Wes, I also decided not to abandon him. No one forced me to stick around, and antagonizing him when he can't talk back sort of undermines that. As much as I'd like to punish him—and plan to once he's regained control of himself—for now, I'll try to be decent.

"Tessa and Grady say hey," I lie, then shake my head. "Okay, you got me. Tessa had some different words for you. She's definitely not a fan. But Grady did specifically instruct me to tell you to wake up. Probably just so he can grill you like he does me every waking second. He's totally obsessed with our Dexid experience. But Tessa and I have been on him to chill out a bit, and I think it's starting to work. He's pulled way back on the drug dealing, which is good. I think we might even be able to convince him to stop all together. He feels responsible for everyone you dosed with Dexid and has some PTSD or something over what could have happened. I've tried to explain to him that your actions weren't his fault but…"

I trail off and bite my lip. It is so hard not to go off on Wes, to just talk to him, even when he can't talk back. "Listen," I say. "I know things are messed up. I know *we're* messed up. I can't tell if I should make small talk or lecture you on all the awful things we've done. Hell, I don't even know if you want me coming here.

"But while I'm pretty sure we're going to have a huge fight as soon as that first word comes out of your mouth, I won't leave you alone, Wes. You've had enough of that, and frankly, it really did a number on you. So I'm sticking around until you wake up. I'm the only person who knows you're not really in a coma and that one of these days, you'll be back."

I stare into his flat, green eyes, searching for the slightest hint of the sparkle that had been such a defining part of his face, but it's not there. I can't stand it.

"I don't imagine we'll ever be friends, and yeah, I know you've got some gripes with me. Well, the feeling's mutual, buddy. So just keep a list. Because as long as you're here, I am too. You said it yourself—we're linked, connected, with or without the drugs, so we might as well suck it up. We'll never shake each other. Whether we like it or not."

I'm quiet for a while, waiting for a response. None comes. Finally, I say, "Your eyes are going to dry out if I keep them open much longer, so I'm going to close them now. But you'll see me again tomorrow." I place my fingers on his eyelids and slide them shut before hopping off the bed and settling into the visitor's chair. I open up a book.

"Now, where were we?" I ask as I turn to a dog-eared page. I clear my throat and begin to read.

I slip my fingers into Wes's hand. To anyone walking by, I

look like a loving girlfriend. Of course, my hand isn't here out of love but pragmatism. I want to know the instant he comes back to life. Because sooner or later, he will.

And I will be ready.

acknowledgments

. . . .

I would like to thank the team at Sourcebooks for being such supportive collaborators—Elizabeth Boyer, Sabrina Baskey, Katy Lynch, Alex Yeadon, Todd Stocke, and Dominique Raccah. Thank you Nicole Komasinski for a beautiful cover. Thank you Steve Geck for bringing me into the fold. And thank you to my editor, Annie Berger, for such thoughtful notes, warm support, and for loving *Jessica Jones*.

Thank you to my favorite agent, Nicole James, and to her cohorts at Chalberg & Sussman.

Thank God for the sanity squad: Sana Amanat, Luz Beltran, Kate Benanti, Mike Carey, Lauren Kogen, Sarah Markley (the namesake), Doreen Mulryan, Zeb Wells, and Alison Sheehy. Thank you Dr. Suraiya Kureshi Haider for dropping the science. And thank you to the Monday morning workshop gang, Diana Asher and Jessica Benjamin.

This book wouldn't exist without my first, last, and every draft in between readers: Stefanie Pintoff and Heather Upton, who are as talented as editors as they are as writers.

Thank you to my big, beautiful family, especially my mom, Julie, and my dad, Ian.

Above all, thank you to my every day crew, without whom nothing would get done. Dan, Phinn, Lyra, and Smudge, you four are the best.

about the author

. . . .

MacKenzie Cadenhead is a trained dramaturg and former comic book editor. She is the author of the middle-grade fantasy novel, *Sally's Bones*, and coauthor of Marvel Press's *Super Hero Adventures* series for young readers. She lives in New York with her husband, son, daughter, and pup.